P9-EIF-230

WITHDRAWN
No longer the property of the
Boston Public Library.
Sale of this material benefits the Library.

INDIGO

Books by Loren D. Estleman

AMOS WALKER MYSTERIES

Motor City Blue
Angel Eyes
The Midnight Man
The Glass Highway
Sugartown
Every Brilliant Eye
Lady Yesterday
Downriver
Silent Thunder
Sweet Women Lie

Never Street
The Witchfinder
The Hours of the Virgin
A Smile on the Face
of the Tiger
Sinister Heights
Poison Blonde*
Retro*
Nicotine Kiss*
American Detective*

The Left-Handed Dollar*
Infernal Angels*
Burning Midnight*
Don't Look for Me*
You Know Who Killed Me*
The Sundown Speech*
The Lioness Is the Hunter*
Black and White Ball*
When Old Midnight
Comes Along*

VALENTINO, FILM DETECTIVE

Frames*
Alone*

Alive!*
Shoot*

Brazen*
Indigo*

DETROIT CRIME

Whiskey River
Motown

King of the Corner
Edsel
Thunder City*

Stress
Jitterbug*

PETER MACKLIN

Kill Zone
Roses Are Dead

Any Man's Death
Something Borrowed,
Something Black*

Little Black Dress*

OTHER FICTION

The Oklahoma Punk
Sherlock Holmes vs.
Dracula
Dr. Jekyll and Mr. Holmes
Peeper

Gas City*
Journey of the Dead*
The Rocky Mountain
Moving Picture Association*
Roy & Lillie: A Love Story*

The Confessions of Al
Capone*

PAGE MURDOCK SERIES

The High Rocks*
Stamping Ground*
Murdock's Law*

The Stranglers
City of Widows*
White Desert*
Wild Justice*

Port Hazard*
The Book of Murdock*
Cape Hell*

WESTERNS

The Hider
Aces & Eights*
The Wolfer
Mister St. John
This Old Bill
Gun Man
Bloody Season

Sudden Country
Billy Gashade*
The Master Executioner*
Black Powder, White
Smoke*
The Undertaker's Wife*

The Adventures of Johnny
Vermillion*
The Branch and the
Scaffold*
Ragtime Cowboys*
The Long High Noon*
The Ballad of Black Bart*

NONFICTION

The Wister Trace

Writing the Popular Novel

*Published by Tom Doherty Associates

LOREN D. ESTLEMAN

INDIGO

A VALENTINO MYSTERY

A TOM DOHERTY ASSOCIATES BOOK

NEW YORK

This is a work of fiction. All of the characters, organizations, and events portrayed in this novel are either products of the author's imagination or are used fictitiously.

INDIGO

Copyright © 2020 by Loren D. Estleman

A Forge Book
Published by Tom Doherty Associates
120 Broadway
New York, NY 10271

www.tor-forge.com

Forge® is a registered trademark of Macmillan Publishing Group, LLC.

The Library of Congress Cataloging-in-Publication Data is available upon request.

ISBN 978-1-250-25835-9 (hardcover)
ISBN 978-1-250-25834-2 (ebook)

Our books may be purchased in bulk for promotional, educational, or business use. Please contact your local bookseller or the Macmillan Corporate and Premium Sales Department at 1-800-221-7945, extension 5442, or by email at MacmillanSpecialMarkets@macmillan.com.

First Edition: 2020

Printed in the United States of America

0 9 8 7 6 5 4 3 2 1

In memory of Richard S. Wheeler,
an immortal writer;
a lifelong friend

I

APPOINTMENT
WITH DANGER

1

HARRIET SAID, "BUT you've seen it a thousand times."

"A gross exaggeration," said Valentino.

"Okay, nine hundred and ninety-nine. On TV, on silver nitrate, celluloid, VHS, Beta—"

"Enough about Beta. Haven't you ever made a mistake?"

"—LaserDisc, DVD, Blu-ray, digital HD; you even followed it frame-by-frame and line-by-line in the pages of the Film Classics Library. Val, during intimate moments you shout out, 'Play, it, Sam!' Why would you want to watch it again on such a special occasion?"

"Everyone should see a classic film at least once on a full-size screen in a public theater, with an audience. That's how it was intended originally."

She jumped on that. "You've seen it that way too, in that art house in Glendale. You geeked out when one of those two girls sitting in front of us whispered to her friend, 'I bet she doesn't show up at the train station.'"

"Well, I want to do that again tonight. Seeing *Casablanca*

with someone who's never seen it before is like watching it for the first time all over again."

Harriet Johansen stood in the middle of The Oracle's auditorium, sweeping her arms to encompass the motion picture palace's gilded and velvet-swagged trim, its mythic statuary and plush brocade. "Why not here? You've spent a fortune restoring this barn. Save it for the grand opening. That's what you and I are celebrating, after all: the butt of the last contract laborer on its way out the door, after five years."

"Nearer six. We met here, remember."

"How could I forget? You, me, and a forty-year-old corpse in the basement. Could it be more romantic?"

"Beats hooking up on a dating app."

She smiled, removed her short silk cape, baring her shoulders, slung it around his neck, and went up on tiptoe to kiss him. Then she pulled back to study his face. "Seriously, what's wrong with here?"

Valentino shook his head. "It'd be anticlimactic after Grauman's screened the same film. Who'd bother to see it again so soon?"

"You, for one." She stopped smiling. "Val, are you putting off actually opening this place to the public?"

"Think you know me, do you?"

"I know I know you. Answer the question."

"Okay, I'm a little nervous. What if no one comes?"

"You built it. They'll come."

His eyes rolled. "That's terrible."

"Now you know what it's like to hang out with you."

"I just need a little more time—to plan the campaign, I mean. You can't just throw open the doors and expect people to come pouring in like Black Friday at Macy's."

"Okay, you win." She retrieved her cape and put it back on.

"But as long as we're all dressed up, let's stop someplace for a drink on the way."

"I'll get my wallet. They're still carding me in my thirties."

"Stop complaining. Your youthful good looks are what attracted me to you in the first place."

"You know, deep down, you're quite shallow."

He took the hidden stairs to his apartment in the projection booth. For years Valentino had lived among the wreckage of old Hollywood, commuting between The Oracle and UCLA, where he supervised the hunt for and restoration of lost motion pictures for the Film & Television Archive. The rest of the time—that time he didn't spend with Harriet—he fought with painters, plasterers, plumbers, electricians, inspectors, and his prima donna of an architect. At long last the work was finished—most of it, anyway—and they'd planned this night on the town to commemorate the event.

Harriet was parked in a tow-away zone in front of the theater. The sun visor was tipped down on the driver's side, showing the word POLICE in block letters. "Shame on you," Valentino said. "You're a forensic pathologist. What's the hurry? All the people you make appointments with are dead. Anyway, you punched out two hours ago."

"Oh, like you never snuck into the screening room at work to watch the Three Stooges on company time."

"Their contribution to slapstick cinema—" He fell back against his seat as she peeled away from the curb.

They went east on Broadway. Vintage movie houses rolled past, their names spelled out in neon and incandescent lights: The Million Dollar, The Orpheus, The Pantages, now advertising Spanish-language features for the largely Hispanic local population. By some miracle, a city of restless bulldozers had overlooked this slice of old California. He went there often for architectural inspiration and nostalgia; but much of the neighborhood was crumbling. He'd turned to point out that they had missed Grauman's Chinese Theatre by many blocks when she drew up before the terra-cotta façade of a five-story building older than most of its neighbors and cut the engine.

"Seriously?" he said. "Aren't we a little overdressed for a mugging?"

"Need I remind you, Merton of the Movies, that more classic films and TV shows have been shot in the Bradbury Building than almost any other place in town? Especially crime stories, which are your favorite."

"But it's no place to order a drink! It's all offices."

"Well, maybe we'll find a bottle of Old Grand-Dad in some shamus' desk drawer." She opened the door and swung her feet to the ground. He got out and followed her to the entrance, feeling more than usually self-conscious in a well-pressed suit and polished shoes.

But he looked forward to revisiting the Bradbury. In his younger days, before Harriet, before The Oracle, before he had any standing in the university, he'd gone there with a sack lunch just to sit in the foyer and watch ghosts. Thanks to the casting departments of Warner Brothers, Paramount, and RKO, generations of hard-boiled detectives and sadistic racketeers had prowled its halls, leaving their shimmering silver essence behind.

Its exterior was unobtrusive, almost anonymous; practically the only note of character was a plaque assigning it to the National Register of Historic Places. But inside lay a breathtaking display of Gay Nineties splendor: tessellated floors, ceramic fixtures, filigreed stairs that climbed up and up a series of railed balconies, the iconic cage elevator, all visible from ground level

I think I'm in a frame. . . . I'm going in there now to look at the picture.
—Robert Mitchum, *Out of the Past* (1947) written by Geoffrey Homes (Daniel Mainwaring)

because of the air shaft that shot straight to the skylight, prisming California sunshine into old-time Technicolor.

Was it still pristine, or had the carrion-birds of Civic Improvement gutted it to attract orthodontists, CPAs, and designers of web sites? Valentino opened the door for Harriet, feeling as he did so a chill of anticipation mixed with dread.

"Surprise!"

The lobby—ornate and unchanged—was packed with familiar faces. Professor Kyle Broadhead, the venerable director of the film preservation department, shared space with his young bride, Fanta; Henry Anklemire, the high-pressure PR rep in charge of UCLA's Information Services; some technicians Valentino had befriended in the lab where films were rescued and restored; and Leo Kalishnikov, the genius (and didn't he know it!) architect in charge of returning The Oracle to its Roaring Twenties glory.

Harriet applauded. "Perfect!"

"Keep quiet, wait till the door opens, yell 'Surprise,'" Broadhead said with a shrug. "Pretty hard to screw that up; although I did worry that Val might overhear Kalishnikov's getup from a block away."

The architect beamed, as if he'd been paid a compliment. Silver-haired and gaunt, he stood apart from the party-clad crowd in a white double-breasted tuxedo, borsalino hat tipped low over his left ear, and a full-length velour cape, red to match his hatband and shoes. "I made a special trip to my tailor in London just for this occasion." The Russian's accent today was pure Sergei Eisenstein; it came and went according to his fancy.

Broadhead said, "And still they let you back in the country."

Valentino turned to Harriet. "So, no *Casablanca*?"

"We'll always have *Casablanca*." She turned. "How long have we been planning this, Fanta?"

The younger woman rested a hand on Broadhead's arm. She was his former student and now his wife—against all odds, given the professor's long solitary widowhood and the age gap. They were unabashedly devoted to each other. "We started talking about it the first time Val threw the main switch. We were interrupted by the fire engines."

"The blaze was not unexpected," her husband added. "What *was*, was me still being around to attend this soiree. The Great Wall didn't take as long or exceed the budget by as much."

Henry Anklemire, his chubby little frame swathed in a faded purple smoking jacket, snorted. "Baloney. You'll bury us every one. You're an excrement of the university."

"*You're* an excrement of the university," said Broadhead. "I'm an ornament. By the way, which long-dead thespian is responsible for that horse blanket you have on?"

"David Niven. Wardrobe department at United Artists will never miss it. This was in one of the pockets: Bonus." He pointed to his obvious toupee.

"I didn't know Niven made a Davy Crockett movie. Ouch!"

Fanta squeezed Broadhead's biceps. "Down, Kyle. This is Val's night."

"Yes, dear." He pried himself loose, rubbing the sore spot, and turned to a rolling cart laden with bottles and trays of hors d'oeuvres. From a gleaming copper ice bucket he plucked a magnum of champagne, swaddled the neck in a linen napkin, and began untwisting the wire that secured the cork. "No celebration is complete without dehydrated gray cells and toxic acetaldehyde surging from your liver."

"A hangover, to the non-biologist," Harriet said. "You've been stepping out on your specialty, Yoda."

"Purely in its interest. I've come to the chapter in my magnum opus on the history of cinema where I dissect *The Lost Weekend*, *The Thin Man*, and *When a Man Loves a Woman*. Our esteemed dean has suggested the title 'A Dissertation on Dipsomania,' but rather than induce coma among my dozens of readers I shall call it 'You're Out of Scotch.'" The cork shot out with an ear-splitting pop and struck a chord off an iron railing. He stanched the flow of bubbly with the napkin, filled a series of crystal flutes, passed them around, kept one for himself, and lifted it. "To the *Titanic,* the *Hindenburg*, New Coke, and The Oracle: four disasters in declining order of casualties."

"Kyle!"

"Very well, my dear. I raise my glass in honor of bold enterprise and devotion to lost glamour, however misdirected."

"Better, lover. Still not good." She drank.

The film archivist sipped, raised his eyebrows. "This is fine. I thought you bought all your liquor in Tijuana."

"Too much trouble now that a passport is required. Mine expired while I was in a cell in Yugoslavia. Anyway, the occasion is stellar. How often does a man manage to outrun *all* his creditors?"

"The jury's still out on that; but thank you."

Broadhead set down his drink. "Reserve your gratitude for when it's appropriate." He walked around behind the cart, drawing everyone's attention to a sheet-covered rectangle resting on an easel; Valentino had been only half aware of it, dismissing it as part of a repair project, common to old structures of historic importance.

Fanta leaned in close to the guest of honor. "He's been busting to show you this for days. I had to promise him sexual favors to hold off."

Valentino grimaced. "Thank you for that image."

A tasseled cord hung alongside the drapery. Broadhead,

standing next to it, took hold of this, paused, and tugged hard. The cloth slid to the floor without interruption.

A hush followed, shattered by spontaneous applause.

"Oh, my." Valentino stared. "Oh, my."

2

IT WAS AN oil painting in a Deco frame, a portrait of a stunningly beautiful woman, rendered by an artist of rare talent. Her cascade of raven hair caught the light in haloes as if she were standing directly across from Valentino. A naked shoulder was opalescent. The eyes—part defiant, part fragile—were a bewitching shade of hazel; they lacked only the addition of a green scarf to turn them to jade. The lips were full and exquisitely shaped. It was a face without flaws.

There wasn't a sound in the room. Even Anklemire, far from the most sensitive soul in attendance, stood mute, his glass raised halfway to his lips and motionless.

"Laura." The name came out in a whisper, as if Valentino had spoken in church.

"The same," said Broadhead, "yet different. When Rouben Mamoulian was signed to direct, he commissioned his wife to paint this picture. Gene Tierney posed for it in person. But it isn't the one everyone remembers from *Laura*. When Otto Preminger came on to replace Mamoulian, he rejected it. I gather it had something to do with her gaze set in the wrong direction; wrong,

I suspect, because it wasn't directed at Preminger. Anyway he had a studio photograph blown up and air-brushed to resemble a painting. That one's unavailable, and if it were, it would be beyond most people's means. This one is dear enough, but because it's less well-known, the price was far more reasonable."

"Even so, Kyle, you can't possibly afford this."

"Right you are. We ornaments of the university are vastly overrated and notoriously underpaid. But *he* can."

Valentino turned to follow the direction of Broadhead's pointing finger. From a corner he'd have sworn was deserted only moments earlier stepped an elegant-looking old man, with white hair fine as sugar combed back from his forehead, very brown skin, and eyes the color of mahogany. His thin build created an impression of height; in fact he was only slightly taller than Anklemire, but a creature from an entirely different species. His evening clothes were silk, the jacket and trousers midnight blue, the shirt snow-white, and his black patent leather shoes glistened like volcanic glass. He was ancient, but erect, and his smile was both genuine and modest.

"*Señor* Bozal!"

The smile broadened. "You remember me. Swell!"

Valentino took the slim brown hand that was offered him. Although the fingers were bony, his grip was firm and dry.

"How could I not? The party you threw to commemorate your gift to my department was almost as lavish as the donation itself. Wherever did you find a cache of George Hurrell's studio stills no one had seen in eighty years?"

"No comment. An old mug like me needs his secrets."

Ignacio Bozal's habitual use of forties-era urban slang, so much in contrast with his Castilian accent, surprised and amused everyone who met him for the first time: He looked like a Spanish grandee and talked like a combination of Allen Jenkins and Broderick Crawford.

Twenty years before immigrating to the United States, he'd suddenly appeared in Acapulco with a bankroll big enough to buy and renovate a broken-down resort hotel and open for business just before the birth of the Mexican Riviera. His American investors accepted his claim that he'd been a silent partner in a gold mine somewhere in the Sierras; but then they'd profited too greatly from the association to press for specifics.

Valentino, whose department was so much richer for Bozal's contributions, was similarly inclined.

"The minute I heard about this shindig, I decided to crash the gate. But I ain't so rough around the edges I'd come empty-handed." The old man gestured toward the painting.

"It's too generous," Valentino said. "I've done nothing to justify such a present."

"Maybe not. But you will, if we can come to a deal."

The old man's gentle appearance was reassuring; it was his underworld vernacular that lent a sinister interpretation to the remark. On a soundstage, the camera operator would dolly in for a close-up of his enigmatic expression just before fading out.

Harriet, who had stopped at one glass of champagne and made free with the canapés, drove. Laura, cocooned in the sheet that had veiled her, rode in the back seat. The theaters were dark at that hour, and the streetlamps, spaced farther apart there than in the busier neighborhoods, illuminated Harriet's profile in flickers.

"How old do you think Bozal is?" she said.

Valentino came out of a half-doze; he'd stopped at one canapé and made free with the champagne. "Based on what little is known of his history, my guess is he's approaching the century mark, not that you'd know it to look at him."

"How much *do* you know about his history?"

"I told you where he says he got his capital. Personally, it sounds a little too close to *The Treasure of the Sierra Madre*. Did you notice the way he talks?"

"How could I miss it? It's like Dick Tracy marinated in Cesar Romero."

"When he came to this country, the TV airwaves were jammed with sports, soap operas, and old movies. He didn't follow sports, and the soaps weren't his cup of tea, so he learned his English from films Hollywood considered too old to re-release to theaters, so they dumped them on television. His preference happened to run to gangster movies. Anyway, that's his story."

"What's yours?"

"I don't have one, but any man who comes out of nowhere with a bundle is bound to attract rumors: He made his stake harboring Nazi war criminals in Brazil, or was a member of the Perón government in Argentina, where he looted the treasury."

They entered West Hollywood, where the glow of the thousands of bulbs that illuminated the marquee of The Oracle were visible for blocks. After decades of darkness, it pleased him to come home to a dazzling display. Kyle Broadhead, less romantic, referred to it as "a human sacrifice to the gaping maw of Consolidated Edison."

"You don't think there's any truth to the rumors, do you?" Harriet said.

"Of course not. In the absence of evidence, people will go to any lengths to provide a substitute; and they never gossip about the basic goodness of Man."

She smiled. "I like that you believe that. So why do you like crime thrillers so much?"

"When I feel blue, I watch Fred Astaire dancing with Ginger Rogers. When I feel naughty, I watch Lawrence Tierney plotting a murder with Claire Trevor. The first cheers me up; the second keeps me from acting on my baser instincts."

"'Baloney,' to quote Henry Anklemire. What's this deal Bozal was talking about, in return for the painting? You were off in a corner together, whispering like a couple of heisters."

He laughed, hiccupped; excused himself. "Two minutes with him and you sound like Bonnie Parker. He's invited me to his house tomorrow morning."

"That sounds like more of a favor for you than for him."

"He was cagy about it, but from some broad hints he made I gather he's come into a film that shouldn't be screened except by someone who knows how to manage old stock. Of course he has a home theater, and of course it will make The Oracle look like an all-night grindhouse in San Diego."

"Doubt that."

"I wouldn't rule anything out where Bozal is concerned. He's one of the biggest private collectors in the business. If I play my cards right, I'll pick up some tips on how he manages to find such treasures without the resources of a major university behind him."

"Greedy. You've already got Laura."

"Told you I have baser instincts."

They pulled up in front of the Baroque/Italianate/ Byzantine pile of sandstone, with bulbs chasing up, down, and around the towering marquee: GRAND OPENING SOON, read the legend in foot-high letters.

"How are you feeling tonight?" Her brows were arched. "Blue or naughty?"

"Inebriated as a North American mammal of the weasel family." He got out, stumbling, opened the back door, and leaned in to retrieve the portrait.

She alighted from her side. "You'd better let me carry that. You're liable to trip and put your head through it, and then you'll feel like Abbott and Costello."

3

Court Street was old town, wop town, cook town, any town. It lay across the top of Bunker Hill and you could find anything there from down-at-heels ex-Greenwich-villagers to crooks on the lam, from ladies of anybody's evening to County Relief clients brawling with haggard landladies in grand old houses with scrolled porches, parquetry floors, and immense sweeping banisters of white oak, mahogany and Circassian walnut.

THAT WAS HOW Raymond Chandler, the great (and unabashedly politically incorrect) detective-story pioneer had described the place in his own time. His works had poured the foundation for film *noir*, Ignacio Bozal's crash course on English as a second language, and incidentally Valentino's guiltiest pleasure. Some of these dark forays into the abnormal psychology of crime had been based on Chandler's novels and stories, others were filmed directly from his screenplays; most of the rest bore his influence.

Although Valentino knew the neighborhood well—and as recently as last night's celebration in the Bradbury Building—

he looked forward to returning as a guest of its most famous resident.

There's nothing rarer than an East L.A. millionaire. That paradox was enough in itself to pique the film archivist's interest, without the added incentive of an invitation to screen some mysterious property possibly lost for generations. Together, they'd compelled him to cancel his day's appointments and brave the gangs and carjackers who preyed upon the honest residents to pay the old man a visit.

There, scorning the mansions of Bel-Air and Beverly Hills, Ignacio Bozal had bought a city block of modest houses in the largely Mexican-American suburb of Los Angeles. A wall went up around it, sheltering his middle-aged children, grown grandchildren, and great-grandchildren under his benevolent eye. He'd kept the largest home for himself and converted it to make room for his various collections; an example of one of which boated into the curb in front of The Oracle and blew a horn that played the first four notes of the *Dragnet* theme.

"Boated" sprang to mind the moment Valentino pushed through the brass-framed front door to the sidewalk: The car was more than twenty feet long, most of its length belonging to the hood, which resembled the visor of a medieval knight's helmet. The cup-shaped headlights were encased in gleaming chromium to match wheel covers the size of hula hoops, and the paint was two-tone, liquid black and royal purple, baked on in so many coats it made a man dizzy staring into the depths of his own reflection.

The next surprise was the driver. Such a rig suggested a chauffeur in livery. Instead, Bozal himself leaned across the front seat from behind the wheel to swing open the door on the passenger's side. He was dressed casually in an old rust-colored suede jacket, threadbare at the elbows, faded jeans, penny loafers, and a billed cap bearing the logo of what his guest suspected belonged to a Mexican baseball team: a rattlesnake coiled around a bat, with a cigar in its mouth.

"Bugatti Type 'forty-one," he said as they peeled away from the curb, the motor churning like a powerful dynamo beneath the country block of hood. "The Royale. Only seven ever made, back in 'thirty-one. The kings of Spain and Belgium each had one. That year I had a bike that blew a tire before I rode it the distance from the rear bumper to the front; not that I ever saw one of these babies then."

Valentino felt swaddled in rich aromatic leather. The old man was a skilled driver, careful but confident. The white-enamel elephant attached to the radiator cap remained rock-steady in the center of the lane. The scenery slid by precisely at the speed limit, according to the gauge in the padded dash. This was what it must have been like to ride in a first-class cabin on the Twentieth Century Limited.

Nearing Bunker Hill, enough of the Victorian homes were still standing to help Chandler find his bearings, but he'd have been nonplussed by the high-rise buildings that had sprung up to cast their shadows on the spires and turrets. They crossed into East L.A., passing Mexican restaurants, corner markets, and long stretches of cinder block sporting gaily colored murals, then purred to a stop before an iron gate in a stucco wall sprayed all over with graffiti. Bozal tilted his head toward the peace signs, hallucinogenic images, and aerosol text in two languages.

"Kids, they gotta have whatchacallit artistic release. I don't mind it, 'cause I'm behind it." He punched the horn.

After a short interval the gate opened and a young Hispanic man in a tailored gray uniform stepped outside. Blue-white teeth shone in a brown face. "Hi, Grandpapa!"

"We have a guest, Ernesto."

"*¡Sí!* Welcome, *señor.*" He stood aside and they cruised through the opening.

The compound reminded Valentino of a barrio scene in *Border Crossing*: tawny children in baggy swimsuits frolicking in the spray from an open fire hydrant, substantially built women in light summer dresses sitting on porches, sleek-haired *hombres* in bright sport shirts smoking cigarettes and conversing in rapid Spanish on the sidewalks. There was plenty of family resemblance to go around. His host had established a colony of his own north of the border, a modern-day Cortez expanding his influence deep into gringo country.

At the end of the block they turned into a circular driveway paved with limestone around a gushing fountain. A motionless parade of exotic automobiles parked bumper-to-bumper formed a horseshoe around the edge. The guest knew little about makes and models, but he was aware that the low-slung convertibles, bus-shaped sedans, high-centered horseless carriages, and slab-sided hardtops covered the history of the motorcar from early days to the Kennedy years. They were enameled in canary yellow, emerald green, candy-apple red, cerulean blue, and gunmetal gray, and all glistening as if they'd been run through a gigantic dishwasher and dipped in molten wax.

"Overflow," Bozal said, pulling up behind a seven-passenger touring car straight out of the original *Scarface* (it might well have been in the movie, at that) and setting the brake. "I knocked down five bungalows to make room for a garage and it still wasn't big enough. I'm waiting for my granddaughter next door to get hitched, then I'll doze her place and build on. Her fiancé's got a job waiting in Omaha, for cat's sake. Maybe I'll get some good steaks out of the deal."

The house was the biggest in the compound, although it was by no means palatial; its owner seemed to have had more interest in obtaining room to display his treasures than to loll in the lap of luxury.

"Hello, Grandfather." A woman in her twenties, pretty but pouty-looking, opened the front door. She wore a red dress, modest in design, but her trim figure, lustrous black hair, and healthy flush under olive-colored skin made it provocative.

Bozal introduced Valentino. "Esperanza, my granddaughter. Not the one who's deserting me for the Nebraska wilderness. I offered to put her through college, but she insists on working her way to a master's; in communications, no less. She could be head curator of the Motion Picture Hall of Fame, but she wants to produce a news show on cable."

"CNN," she clarified. "C-SPAN would be my next choice. Movies are my grandfather's thing, not mine; but he's forgiven me so far as to pay me three times the going wage for answering the door and taking visitors' coats." Despite her solemn expression, a merry light glimmered in her eye. Valentino saw something more than idle mischief when their gazes met; but he was off the market: a mantra worth repeating. She swiveled aside for them to pass.

"What's your poison?" Bozal took up a post behind a sleek white bar with a wall-size mirror at his back. The glittering display of liquor bottles and stemmed glasses slung upside-down from the ceiling might have belonged to a gangster boss's lair on a 1940s soundstage.

"It's early for me, thanks."

"You ain't had practice." He poured amber liquid from a cut-glass decanter into a tumbler, squirted in seltzer, and carried his drink down into a sunken living room.

The room was done in neutral tones, a sharp contrast to the warm, vibrant colors that decorated the rest of the neighborhood. It was like stepping from bright glare into shade. The chairs and sofas were upholstered in cushy leather. Above the mantel hung a portrait of a woman with the proud features of a Spanish patrician. She wore jet buttons in her ears and a plain blouse cut low to show off her shoulders. It was as haunting as the painting now in Valentino's possession, the original center-piece for the film *Laura*.

Bozal saw the cast of his glance. "Estrella, my wife. I lost her fifty years ago. Damn careless, if you ask me."

"I'm sorry."

"Don't be. She wouldn't know regret if it bit her on the nose. She's responsible for everything you lay eyes on here. All I did was supply the juice. Wasn't for her, I'd be one of them para-sites you see in the country clubs, palling around with cheap broads in expensive perfume." He lifted his glass to the image and sipped.

"But why East L.A.?"

"Might as well ask why Beverly Hills? There, I'd be just a spick with money, probably earned pushing drugs; a racist neighbor with unlimited credit is still a son of a bitch in a sheet. Here, I'm part of the community, something bigger than me."

They sat facing each other in matching armchairs.

"I can't thank you enough for Laura," Valentino said. "It will occupy the place of honor in the lobby of The Oracle."

"Just don't fall in love with it. That gag only works in movies, and then only through the closing credits. The audience rips it apart on the way home."

"Not *Laura*."

Bozal aimed a porcelain smile over the edge of his glass. It was as vaguely sinister as his eccentric use of the English lan-guage. "Okay, sure. But lay off the thanks till you see my end of the deal. You may want to give it back."

4

HARRIET WAS WRONG.

Partially, anyway. While the theater Bozal had installed in the lower level of his home didn't make The Oracle look like a dump tailor-made for showing barely acceptable features, it outstripped the grandest screening rooms commissioned by major movie stars and most neighborhood picture houses.

He'd taken a larger-than-average basement, extended it under his multi-car garage, and hired a team of contractors to turn it into something Valentino could describe only as an underground mall: what seemed miles of tiled hallway passed a replica of a 1930s automobile showroom, complete with Depression-era models in mint condition on display, brightly gleaming, a mid-century-type service station built of white glazed brick with a black 1955 Porsche pulled up to the pumps—waiting, it seemed, for James Dean to bring the engine to life and speed toward his date with destiny—and a men's haberdashery stocked with mannequins decked out in vests, double-breasted suits, and snappy fedoras, decorated with patriotic posters advertising war bonds to fight the Axis.

Their way led at last to the theater itself, a plush Art Moderne palace lit by wall sconces, with stadium seating to accommodate two dozen viewers and gold velvet curtains cloaking a screen with a stage for live performances between shows.

"It's magnificent," was all the visitor could find to say.

"You should've seen it when I bought the place. The previous owner hosted cockfights down here. His neighbors turned him in. He needed quick money to pay his lawyer, so I got it for a song. 'Course, more excavation and the retrofitting ate up the difference. Let's go see the projection booth."

A door concealed in the molding led up a short flight of stairs into a square chamber with walls of plain concrete. It contained an ultramodern laser projector mounted to the ceiling and a black steel giant resembling a locomotive. It had reels the size of platters and a threading system as complicated as the Gordian knot.

Valentino goggled at this. "Is that a 'forty-four Bell and Howell?"

"'Forty. I scored it in a junk shop in Tehuantepec, where it'd been busy collecting dust and mouse turds for sixty years. Took me another ten to track down replacement parts from all over the world. I had to buy a shut-down theater in Prague just to get the lens assembly. Outfit in Detroit made the arc lamp from scratch; Bausch and Lomb the reflector mirror. I lucked out on the mechanic. He was retired, living right down there in the Valley. He'd never worked on a projector before, but it's just a series of simple machines, going back to the Greeks."

"How big is your silver-nitrate collection?"

"Big enough. But I went to all that bother for just one."

Bozal turned and took a pizza-size film can off a steel utility rack. "Ever hear of a mug named Van Oliver?"

The abrupt question surprised Valentino. Plainly the old man had little patience for small talk. "Old-time picture actor.

He was murdered, supposedly. Another one of Hollywood's unsolved mysteries."

His host jerked his chin, approving. Aged and slight as he
was—his gold Rolex and cuff links looked too heavy for his fragile wrists—all his movements were steady and his eyes bright as
a bird's. "That's refreshing. Most people don't know Van Oliver
from Oliver Hardy."

"We can't all be buffs. Most people wouldn't know him. He
only made one movie, and it—" He stopped, looking at the can.
He felt the old familiar thrill.

Bozal's smile was wicked. It was the privilege of rich men to
carry suspense to the brink of cruelty. "Officially, he just disappeared. My bet is they buried him up in the hills, or rowed
him out past Catalina and dumped him overboard in a cement
overcoat. In those days, you couldn't convict anyone of murder in the state of California without a corpse. I guess the law
didn't want to fry someone just because someone else decided
to take a powder and forgot to tell anyone, but it sure sold a lot
of shovels and quicklime."

"It was almost a double murder, if you can apply the term to
a movie studio," said Valentino. "He'd been getting the kind of
star treatment they reserve for major properties: elocution lessons, tailors, a big flashy car, dates with glamour queens, and an
army of press agents, so he could make a splash during interviews and premieres. Only he couldn't, because he died before
the film was released. They shelved it. That was the end of
RKO."

"Helped by that nut Howard Hughes. Sooner or later he
drove everything he owned into the ground. You can't keep hir-
ing and firing and quadrupling budgets and stay in business.
Lucy told me the best day in her life was the day she bought the
studio, four years after RKO fired her."

"You knew Lucille Ball?"

"Through Desi. In those days the Spanish colony in Hollywood was thick as thieves."

Valentino had never met anyone closely connected with *I Love Lucy*, Desi Arnaz, and the birth of Desilu Studios.

"That was in 'fifty-seven," Bozal said. "They might have recut and reshot the picture to build up one of the other players and brought it out later, but the *noir* cycle was on its last legs. Welles's *Touch of Evil* came out the next year and tanked."

He snarled out the side of his mouth. "Universal butchered *Evil* in post-production; shoved Welles right off the cliff, so of course it under-performed. Nothing's changed in sixty years except the suits. Anyway, the Oliver vehicle went the same way as its star. Nobody gave a rat's behind about preservation then. Re-release was strictly for proven properties, the studios had already sold their old libraries to television, and there was no video. Desilu edited down the script to an hour for TV, but none of the networks would touch it, even with a new cast. In this town a bad rep has a half-life of a hundred years. You know the title?"

"*Bleak Street*," Valentino said. "Oliver played a racketeer loosely based on Bugsy Siegel. Only he didn't play him the way pioneer actors played gangsters in the thirties. The few insiders who saw the dailies said he had an entirely new take on the character. If the movie had been allowed to open, it would have revolutionized the crime film the way *The Godfather* did fifteen years later."

"Not just crime pictures. Acting; only it didn't seem like acting. Edward G. Robinson was nasty, Paul Muni a goon, Jimmy Cagney was like a bomb about to go off. Oliver was entirely natural; you wouldn't know he was reading lines. Also it's clear no stunt doubles were used for his fight scenes. It wasn't like watching a movie, more like something happening right in front of you, that you might be sucked into any time: disturbing, which was ideal for the form. There was even a rumor he wrote the screen-play himself under a pseudonym, or at least made changes in the text. The plot had all the usual clichés, but I'd stand the production up beside anything else out there."

As he warmed to his subject, Bozal's speech shifted away from street lingo toward more formal language, using jargon familiar to any story conference. Clearly the old man's passion outstripped his affectations. What was more to the point, he wasn't parroting something he'd read or heard; he spoke as someone who'd seen the evidence firsthand. The shock of hope Valentino had felt settled into a cozy hum. He had little doubt now what was in the can.

He wondered if he was a latent masochist. He put off asking the question that was foremost on his mind. Instead he drew out the excruciating pleasure of suspense.

"What made everyone so certain he was killed? Sudden success can be terrifying. Maybe he just dropped out of sight because he couldn't take the pressure. It was easier then to re-locate and make up a new identity."

"His kind thrives on pressure; enduring it as well as apply-ing it. How do you think he did such a good job capturing a gangster's personality? He came here from New York to work for Mickey Cohen, the local mob boss."

"Doing what?"

"Bodyguard; not that the little twerp needed one. He already had an army on the job. He thought surrounding himself with muscle made him look like a bigger shot than he was. Some folks said Oliver got bored with sitting around Mickey's house in Brentwood watching Roy Rogers and started making hits on the side."

"Sounds like typical Hollywood hokum."

"Probably. That last part anyway. But he'd been seen around town with Mickey, shooting golf and picking up dames in night-clubs. When the *Bleak Street* hype started, the attention got to be too much for his employers. They were camera shy after so many big-time operators got themselves deported or shut up for tax evasion. They cut their losses same way they did with Bugsy Siegel back in 'forty-seven, only by then they'd learned not to be so public about it."

Valentino banked his fires. His profession had taken him close to criminal territory before, and he hadn't enjoyed the experience. "How much of this is likely and how much gossip?"

Bozal tented his shoulders, let them drop. "In this town, who can say? Is there any other place so visible, yet so frequently out of focus?" He drummed his fingers on the edge of the film can.

His guest couldn't hold out any longer. "Where'd you find it?"

5

"**RETIRED FILM EDITOR** died last year; he was there when RKO changed hands. I bought his estate."

"Don't tell me. You bought it all just to get that one item."

"No, there were some outtakes from a couple of Astaire-Rogers musicals and six minutes of the original *Untouchables* nobody's seen in fifty years; also a Movieola machine in cherry condition and a box of cutting and splicing tools. I sold the tools to a collector for five times what they were worth. I usually make money on these deals. Heck, I unloaded that theater in Prague to Hilton."

"I can't believe I missed a sale like that. What was the editor's name?"

"You wouldn't recognize it. He was out before the industry gave negative cutters screen credit. It was a private deal in Europe."

Valentino was certain this rapid-fire response was a lie. Shrewd as he was, Bozal lacked the imagination to make up a name for his mysterious source that would convince a fellow traveler. Most likely he was protecting a favorite fishing hole.

"You have the negative?"

"No such luck. Studio security never let those out of their sight, even when the high exalted muckety-mucks decided against release. He probably remastered the film, made a fresh positive, and smuggled it out in the confusion during the change in management. When you think of how much contraband managed to walk off those lots over the years—"

Valentino broke under pressure. "Just to be clear, sir; it's *Bleak Street* we're talking about?"

The old man showed no offense at the interruption. He smiled and scooped a telephone handset from its niche in the wall. "Esperanza."

Minutes later the attractive young Hispanic woman entered the booth. Her simple red sheath and modest heels accentuated the contours of her muscular (but by no means unfeminine) calves. She directed another brief appraising glance at the visitor, then shifted her attention to her grandfather.

"Mr. Valentino will show you what to do."

"Grandfather, I know how to handle film stock. On top of what you taught me, my teachers gave me a thorough grounding in all aspects of communications technology, even obsolete—"

"*Handling* is precisely what I *don't* want you to do, *niña*. Pay close attention to everything this man says and does. If he isn't satisfied that you can be trusted to carry on in his absence, I'll have to be a rotten host and keep him at work."

However irked she might have been by Bozal's lack of faith in her abilities, she slid her eyes toward the archivist in a way that harbored no animosity; quite the reverse.

Bozal seemed not to notice. Still holding the large flat can, he turned to the archivist. "Is there anything you need that you didn't bring?"

"Depends on what condition the film is in. I have a kit in the car, but if the integrity is compromised in any way, I wouldn't take a chance on screening until the techs have had a chance to examine it back at the lab."

"'Compromised.' The way you guys talk. You'd think it's a dame instead of a movie." Bozal chuckled. "No vinegar stink, no yellowing. A little rust inside one of the original cans, so I had the reels taken out and put in these." He thumped the can, which was made of brushed aluminum and rust-proof.

"Molecular sieves?"

"Yup."

"How about the reels?"

"You tell me. I wouldn't let anyone unwind and rewind the stock onto fresh ones except an expert."

It was Valentino's turn to smile. "Someone's been doing his homework."

"Sure. I didn't just fall off the turnip truck."

"Then I'm ready." Valentino slid a pair of latex gloves from his inside breast pocket.

There were five cans on the rack, each containing a reel. Esperanza was a keen student and a fast learner—all the better for her tutor, who was relieved to break free of her spell early. Throughout the lesson she stood closer than seemed necessary.

He wasn't flattered. There was something impersonal in her frank interest; calculating, as if she'd set herself a challenge, either to annoy the family patriarch or to win some kind of bet, perhaps only with herself. No, there was nothing flattering about the situation. He was spoken for, and had no intention of becoming a notch on someone's belt.

If getting Grandfather's goat was her purpose, it seemed to have failed. He showed no interest in her behavior, or for that matter in the process of managing fragile film. Valentino suspected he knew more about silver-nitrate etiquette than he cared to let on.

So why had he been so eager to invite the film archivist to this private premiere? The man was (in a phrase borrowed from Kyle Broadhead) "a riddle wrapped in a mystery inside an enigma—with a chewy chocolate center."

But this sense of unease fled before the prospect ahead. This was how an archaeologist must feel upon discovering an ancient civilization long thought lost. Descending the steps to the theater, he leaned heavily on the handrail; more so than his elderly host, whose gait remained steady. Valentino had gone rubbery in the knees.

They took center seats facing the curtained screen. Bozal tilted back the top of an armrest, exposing a row of switches and a gridded speaker. "Refreshment? Popcorn, a soda, something with more of a kick? I like to match the drink to the movie, like the right wine with supper. Rum with Fairbanks, champagne with Garbo, beer with Brando."

"And with Oliver?"

Out came the porcelains. "Scotch, straight up."

"Still too early, but thanks."

"You'll never get to be as old as me if you don't start pickling your innards." He flipped a switch. "*?Sí, Abuelo?*" came a youthful male voice from the speaker.

"Can it, Eduardo. You speak English better than all your teachers. Pour me a Dewar's."

Presently a trim, dark-complected boy of twelve or thirteen entered from the hall carrying a tall tumbler on a tray. His blue-black hair was cut close to the scalp and he wore a white tunic buttoned at the shoulder over black chinos, orange Reeboks on his feet. Bozal scooped the glass off the tray and made a sort of magician's gesture with his other hand. A folded twenty-dollar bill had appeared on the tray.

"Thank you, Grandfather."

When he'd left, Valentino asked the old man how many grandchildren he had.

"Eduardo's a *great*-grandchild; and I don't know how many of *them* there are either."

"But you know all their names?"

"I'm lousy at math."

Another switch spread the heavy curtains with a hum, exposing a high-quality screen wide enough to display *Lawrence of Arabia* in all its original glory. He raised the top of the armrest on his other side and lifted a telephone receiver. Valentino overheard Esperanza's voice.

"Ready when you are, I.B.!"

"Cut the comedy and roll the film." He hung up and closed the armrest. "You got any kids?"

"No."

"If you ever do, first time they tell a joke, smack 'em in the kisser."

"That sounds like something from a movie, but I can't place it."

"It's in the second reel. Shush, now. If there's one thing I can't stand it's mugs that yak during the movie."

Bozal threw yet another switch. The lights went down. Valentino's excitement level went up.

6

A **SQUARE BEAM** of light shot through the aperture in the booth and splashed across the screen, followed closely by the clickety-click of celluloid frames clattering through the gate; is there any sound more sweet?

There were a few seconds of blank footage, the lead-in, and then the old familiar countdown began, the letters and numerals jumping due to broken sprocket holes (not enough to damage the film):

10

NINE

8

7

SIX

5

4

3

2

A broadcast tower appeared, sending out animated concentric circles from atop the curvature of the earth, accompanied by Morse code beeps: the RKO Studio logo, in razor-sharp black and white and shimmering silver, illuminating the image as if from behind; an effect missing from features printed on modern safety stock. The picture was square, conforming to the original aspect ratio, the blank screen on both sides masked by the gold velvet curtains.

Now the title pounced onto the screen, with a plosive from the string section, the letters standing out dramatically in pseudo-third dimension, like blocks in a prison wall:

BLEAK STREET

With a sigh, Valentino settled in for seventy-nine minutes of voyeuristic bliss.

His host had been right about the elements of cliché. All the allegorical tropes were in place: the revenge-driven anti-hero, the implausibly patient Good Girl, the poisonous Femme Fatale, the Psycho Villain, and the hapless Squealer, shot to death in a telephone booth whilst informing on his colleagues. *Bleak Street* had, in fact, every disadvantage of a sub-genre on the verge of extinction.

However, superior performances, edge-of-the-seat tension, and a cloying miasma of dread made it anything but run-of-the-mill. Even the gutter dialogue, boiled as hard as a ten-minute egg and too glib for ordinary conversation, came off as naturally as infection settling into a neglected wound.

Van Oliver was the keystone. From the moment he made his entrance, stepping down off a train from New York and pausing, only his eyes moving as he stood on the platform with one hand hidden inside the breast of his trenchcoat, searching for friends or enemies (possibly both in one package), the movie became unique, and all his. He was a lean man in his early twenties, with dark Mediterranean features under the turned-down brim of his fedora, piratically handsome. When he opened his mouth to deliver his first line, Valentino half expected an exotic accent. Pure American came out instead, in a casual baritone that took on a dangerous edge when he met resistance. He acted balletic rings around the veteran cast. It was impossible to take one's eyes off him. Even the scenes in which he didn't appear crackled with tension, actors and audience alike anticipating his return. He seemed to have *star* tattooed on his forehead.

The action scenes—Oliver disarming a rival with one hand, punishing him with a backward swipe of the other, retreating into a pitch-black doorway from the approach of a cruising police car—again with one hand out of sight beneath his coat, ready to commit cold-blooded murder in his obsession with his grim purpose—were exciting and fresh. There was little on-screen violence, however. One of the hallmarks of this school of filmmaking was its sardonic compliance with the stern Hays/Breen censorship code, averting graphic scenes of bloodshed by casting the action in shadow on an alley wall. Like the offstage murder of King Duncan in *Macbeth,* the device compelled the audience to supply the gory details from its imagination, creating a tableau far more disturbing than any special-effects team could create.

This was the form, pure and simple: Spun by writers, directors, actors, and cinematographers from the whole cloth of wartime angst, released in an unbroken chain of mostly second features to feed an insatiable appetite for gritty realism. It was dismissed by critics, censors, and sometimes the creators themselves as pulp, melodrama, sordid trash; even subversive anti-American propaganda. It took a colony of French reviewers, exposed all of a sudden to this fare in one undigested lump at the end of World War II, to give it a name: *cinema noir* (black film). Like so many of America's native contributions to world culture, it could be traced back to foreign lands, smuggled onto our shores by refugee directors from Fascist Europe, introducing the look of German Expressionism, French existentialism, and the nihilistic view of a world gone terribly wrong.

Pools of harsh cold light. Cameras tilted at precarious angles. Shadows cut out as if by a shiv. Rain-slick streets stuck in perpetual midnight. It was all conspiracy, wrought by *auteurs*, scenarists, studio electricians, and second-unit crews to create a nightmare that was still there when you awoke. Desperate characters speeding headlong toward destruction, like a sedan careering down a mountain road with a roadblock at the bottom and the audience riding in the back seat.

The ending riveted. Oliver's death scene was defiant, not contrite, and bore all the earmarks of a life actually expiring on camera, not at all play-acting. His curtain line—"You and what army?"—belonged in any reference book on great movie quotations. It could not have occurred during the gangster cycle of the Depression—the powerful Catholic Anti-Indecency League would never have allowed it—and its lack of inner conflict was a slap in the face to the standard view of 1940s *noir*. Had the picture been released, this drastic departure might have revitalized the genre, extending its existence another twenty years. Valentino found himself applauding when the closing credits appeared.

The lights came up. Ignacio Bozal, lounging now in the adjoining seat with legs crossed, observed his companion's expression with a smirk. "Quite a show, eh? Paul Newman would never have got a shot at *The Left Handed Gun* if Oliver had hung around: All that Actors Studio bunk would've stunk like cheap aftershave next to the real deal. That's why I buy into all that hype about mob connections. You don't pick up that stuff mawking over your little dog getting run over when you were six."

"I don't know if I agree about Paul Newman, but *Bleak Street* could have jump-started the revolution of the sixties ten years early."

"It would also have buried the studio system that much faster. The red-baiters in Washington jumped on any excuse to denounce a picture as pro-Communist; it meant headlines and re-election. The studio moguls didn't know it at the time, but Oliver getting killed was the best thing that could've happened to them. It saved their butts from unemployment and probably indictment."

Valentino pointed to where the credits had faded from the screen. "Whatever happened to Madeleine Nash, the bad girl? She looked familiar."

"She had bits as wisecracking secretaries in a couple of programmers before she landed this part. Her real name was Magdalena Novello; she was Puerto Rican. She could turn the accent on and off. After the picture was shelved, RKO didn't renew her contract. Columbia offered her a long-term deal, but that meant sleeping with Harry Cohn, so she turned it down. I heard she married some joker and moved to Europe."

"Too bad; for moviegoers, I mean. She held her own against Oliver."

"She'd've been out of work in a couple of years anyway. Can you see her as June Cleaver in *Leave It to Beaver*, or teaching a bunch of teenage brats in *Our Miss Brooks*? TV wouldn't have let her play anything else; the FCC was worse than Hays and Breen. Mustn't warp the morals of the little rugrats in their parents' living rooms."

"For someone who came here late in life, you know a lot about inside Hollywood."

The old man blew a raspberry, loud enough for Esperanza to call and ask if he was okay. He said something terse and hung up. "Everybody who was anybody wintered at my joint in Acapulco. You hear a lot of gossip when you play the obliging host. See a lot, too. Marilyn Monroe went skinny-dipping in the pool." He leered.

"Is that how you heard about Van Oliver?"

"Some of it down there, some up here. It's part of industry lore. If there's anything folks in the profession like to talk about, it's scandal, and the nastier the better. He was just what you saw on-screen, though I don't know if there's anything to that rumor about him bumping guys off. He ran errands for the Five Families back East, everyone seemed to agree on that. Maybe he was tagged to babysit Mickey Cohen, or maybe to muscle in on the guilds. Anyway he got his picture taken at the Brown Derby and the Coconut Grove, usually with some hot-to-trot starlet on his arm. Howard Hughes liked his looks and offered him a screen test. Well, you can see the impression he made. The studio changed his name from Benny Obrilenski and signed him for three pictures."

"And the mob saw that as a threat?"

"Maybe they didn't approve of moonlighting, or maybe Oliver fell for his own publicity and told them to go climb a rope. Anyway, when the picture wrapped, so did he."

Valentino pondered. From the direction of the booth, he heard the rapid clicking of reels being rewound. He knew the sound better than the beating of his own heart. Like her grandfather, Esperanza knew more about the proper treatment of volatile silver-nitrate film stock than either would admit. The hospitality of the Bozal household was genuine enough; but as friendly as its residents behaved, inside those walls lurked unspoken thoughts, hidden agendas, and secrets to the ceiling.

one fluent to keep up; thus did he deliver a rebuke for her earlier impertinence and display his superior vocabulary in one stroke. Lips pressed tight, she nodded and made her exit.

He waited until the door closed, then tipped a hand toward the film. "Do with it how you like; give it to your bosses or use it to re-open your playhouse with a bang."

The remark, off-hand as it sounded, shook Valentino head to toe. He was ashamed of all the unworthy things he'd been thinking. He was even prepared to forgive Esperanza for her relentless flirting.

At first he thought he'd misunderstood. At the risk of changing the old man's mind, he said, "You're offering me *Bleak Street,* free of charge?"

His host smiled wearily.

"Please. What would I do with the money, stuff it in my mattress? It's lumpy enough as it is. I don't sleep as good as when I was ninety."

"A rediscovered classic of this quality, and a mysterious disappearance? I can hear our man in Information Services rubbing his hands over the publicity. These days, just unveiling a priceless property isn't enough. You've got to have a brass band and the lead story on Fox News."

"These days, my aunt's fanny. I told you nothing's changed in this town. MGM spent a cool million in 'thirty-eight scouring every beauty pageant, finishing school, and Campfire Girls jamboree in the country looking for an actress to play Scarlett O'Hara, when it had already signed Vivien Leigh; that's a million in *Depression* dollars. Then it was newsreels and fan magazines, now it's a continuous crawl on the bottom of a TV screen. I guess that's what they call progress."

"This gift is beyond generous, *Señor* Bozal. There may be an honorary doctorate in it for you and a seat on the board of regents."

7

BOZAL PICKED UP the telephone handset, which appeared to be a direct line to the projection room. "Finished rewinding?"

"*Sí, Abuelo.* Just putting the last reel in the can."

She was teasing her grandfather. Obviously she'd overheard him upbraiding Eduardo for his Spanish conceit; but he didn't rise to the bait. He seemed to be more permissive with his granddaughter. "Bring 'em all down."

A tense silence—tense for Valentino—fell while they waited. Presently the young woman descended the steps with cans under both arms and at a nod from Bozal stacked them on the vacant seat beside him.

He scowled up at her. "I don't expect the eggheads in that high-dollar school to teach you anything, but don't my lessons count?"

Red spots showed on her dusky cheeks, the first sign she'd given of embarrassment. She muttered an apology and rearranged the cans so that they stood upright, braced by the armrests.

He said something in a flood of Spanish too rapid for even

"*Muchacho*, a spick with a buncha letters after his name is just a wetback with a diploma, and I stopped going to meetings before you were born. Nothing ever gets finished except a lotta pastry." The old man's snicker carried traces of Dan Duryea and Torquemada. "There *is* something you can do for me, and it won't cost you a cent."

Valentino was back on his guard. When someone promised something that "wouldn't cost you a cent," you better be sure you can afford it.

This time he wasn't kept in suspense. "I got some Vatican bigshots stalling over a theme park I want to open in Tuscany, dedicated to classic Italian cinema; I need the Pope's okay to bring the authorities in Rome on board, on account of some of the steamy scenes in *La Dolce Vita* and *Eight and a Half*. I'm this close to swinging a visit by a delegation of Cardinals." He pinched the air. "I know I can win 'em over with a face-to-face on my own turf. An exclusive screening of *Greed* could seal the deal. The flick drips with Old Testament justice; they lap that up. The fact that it was lost for eighty years is a bonus."

"I'll pay for the dupe," he added, when his listener hesitated.

But the brief silence was from shock and relief, not doubt.

"You'll have a print if I have to bootleg it myself," Valentino said.

"God, I love foul play!"

Henry Anklemire leapt up from behind his desk next to the boiler room. As always, "Our man in Information Services" resembled an evil cherub in a toupee a shade too dark for his vintage and a checked suit (size portly), polka-dot tie, and striped shirt that made a cataclysmic statement Valentino thought could not have been coincidental. The little flack had an arrangement (perhaps sexual, perhaps mercenary) with most of the wardrobe mistresses in the industry that kept him supplied with costumes reaching as far back as the slapstick comedies of Hal Roach. His face glowed as from a strong shot of whiskey. So far as the film archivist was aware, he was no lush; he got his highs from the prospects of a successful hype.

"We'll keep that angle between ourselves until we spring it on the public," Valentino said. "The dean thinks Sherlock Holmes was a sociopath."

But there was no stopping Anklemire once he was on a roll.

"Look at Marilyn Monroe; not one-tenth the talent of Billie Holiday, but she had the good sense to get murdered by the Kennedys. You ever see Billie Holiday on a T-shirt?"

"From time to time. It's *Judy* Holliday you're talking about; and the answer is no. In any case you wouldn't know Judy from Jumbo if I hadn't forced you to watch *Born Yesterday* on DVD. Also, there's some question about whether the Kennedys were involved in Marilyn's death."

Anklemire had offered his expertise to the university after a year of retirement on top of forty years of advertising cigarettes, automobiles, and feminine hygiene products for a venerable agency on Madison Avenue, on condition that his salary wouldn't threaten his retirement benefits. Even when the government changed the law to allow unlimited compensation from the private sector without penalty, he hadn't applied for a raise; twelve months of shooting golf and playing canasta with his next-door neighbors in Tarzana had made him desperate for any activity that didn't involve listening to anyone's blow-by-blow account of his prostate operation. The department director had assured him that low pay was no obstacle to his employment.

Most of the academic community loathed the little caricature of a man, for the very reasons the archivist liked him. He was an aggressive promoter who knew the common denominator that shook loose money from every corner of society, and he had no patience for objections based on propriety or prestige. Give him a salable commodity and he'd sell it. He knew nothing about movies or their heritage, but he knew how to turn silver nitrate into gold.

Even Kyle Broadhead, who tolerated him at best, acknowledged that one crass little garden gnome like him was worth twenty "ornaments of the university," as the professor himself had been ordained.

"*Born Yesterday*, great flick. They ought to colorize it." Anklemire's face grew solemn, or as close to it as it ever came. "What you want to do, you want to send the pitcher on tour, book the revival houses, pass the hat for donations. Hey, invite the FBI! They could sponsor the whole *schmear*, tack on a documentary feature about how crime don't pay."

"Henry, J. Edgar Hoover's been dead almost fifty years."

"Sure. I don't just read the trades. Right now, the Bureau can use a boost more than us. You don't win no friends slapping the cuffs on folks just for telling fibs; who'd be left?"

"Not you." Valentino smiled.

"Okay, it's a long shot. Nobody ever gained nothing by not trying. After it's finished the circuit, this—what's it called again?"

"*Bleak Street*."

"Stinko title. Change it. No? Okay, we'll work around it. After it's made the rounds, we lease it to TCM, then bring it out on DVD: Two-disc set, buncha talking heads yakking about what the movie really meant to say, how the lab rats saved it from ruin, yada-yada, that stuff everybody says they care about but nobody watches all the way through, only they buy it, 'cause who'd settle for one when he can have two? This outfit sure can use the cash."

He raised his voice above the banging of the water pipes next door. "What we do to get the media to cooperate is play up

the mysterious-disappearance angle, especially the mob connection; pound it into the ground. That didn't hurt Geraldo one
little bit, even if he did come up with bupkus from Al Capone's
secret vault."

Watching "Angle-worm Anklemire" work himself up to or-
gasm was always entertaining, but as Valentino saw it, part of
his job was to keep him from flying off the rails. "We found a
ground-breaking movie that's been missing for six decades. Isn't
that worth anything?"

"Boring. Strictly third paragraph, bottom of the hour after
the weather. Nobody cares."

"Nobody but the people you and I work for. They're what's
keeping you from sitting around watching *Matlock* with your
fellow inmates in an assisted-living community in Oxnard."

"Which is where'd I be, if I followed that line of reasoning."
His face was grave. When you least expected it, the court jester
took off his cap and bells and assumed all the dignity of a Su-
preme Court justice. "Tell you what, Professor; you do what you
do best and leave me to mine."

To this little man, who liked to brag that he'd been making
his way in the world since dropping out of school at sixteen,
everyone else at the university was a tenured Ph.D.

Valentino was too cowed by this solemn display to put up an
argument on behalf of film history. "What do you need from me?"

"You're the archaeologist. Start digging. I can't write copy
without material."

"Archivist, not archaeologist."

"What's the difference? Do some homework. Interview
people. Get me color: big hats, gun molls, armor-plated Cadil-
lacs, rat-a-tat-tat!" He mimed firing a submachine gun.

Here he was again, the living video arcade; and for the first
time his visitor realized that the buffoonery was a mask. He
used his antics to distract people from the fact that he was as

serious about what he did as anyone else at UCLA, Valentino included. It made people underestimate him and drop their guard just as he moved in for the kill.

"I can't promise much, Henry. *Bleak Street* was shelved in post-production, before the publicity mill could warm up. All I've got is rumors and some inside stories Bozal overheard. Without corroboration, they're useless. The public isn't as ignorant of hype as it was sixty years ago; it wants sensation—dirt, to be blunt. You've got a star with possibly sinister connections who dropped off the face of the earth just as the underworld was consolidating the power it drew from Prohibition. A pro like you could build a campaign as tall as the Watts Tower on a foundation like that. What else could you possibly need?"

Ignacio Bozal had nothing on Henry Anklemire when it came to blowing a juicy raspberry.

"That's prologue, the kind of stuff they used to blow off in whatchacall expository text after the title card and the bill. Nobody goes to the movies to read, for Pete's sake. They want faces, sex, action, the bloodier the better. Forget the on-set baloney. Find somebody who was there and make 'em dish up."

"You're forgetting how long ago this was. Whatever happened to Oliver has found its way to everyone else connected with the picture. There's no hit man like Old Father Time. Wait." An image leapt into the foreground of Valentino's brain. He'd been only vaguely aware of it at the time of exposure. He took out his phone, into which he'd entered all the information he used to keep in notebooks, tapped keys, scrolled.

"Roy Fitzhugh's still with us," he said; "or was when I entered his name here. I saw him in the film, playing a mob henchman. It was an early role, and he had only one line, so he didn't make it into the end credits. I was overwhelmed with the whole package, so it didn't register at the time."

"Fix that. Save being a fan for after quitting, when you're

sitting at home with a bowl of popcorn in your lap. Be a working stiff when you're on the clock."

"I interviewed him last year about a bit he had in *M Squad*. Here it is." He stopped scrolling.

"He must be a hundred."

"Not quite that bad. He always played older than he was. He had one of those faces. I hope his memory's still good."

"Go see him. I'd send a photog with you, but the flash might stop every pump in the joint. Try to keep him on topic. We want to know what happened to this monkey Oliver, not how many football teams Jayne Mansfield slept with."

Valentino laughed. "What do you want me to do, solve his murder?"

"If you can squeeze it in."

8

THE ARCHIVIST WAS still shaking his head when he dropped by the lab to see how the technicians were coming with the film he'd brought back from East L.A.

"Why are you shouting?" Jack Dupree, an uncommonly handsome young man with a gleaming shaven onyx head, squinted as if against bright sun. He wore a yellow Haz-Mat suit, minus the sci-fi hood and latex gloves, which he'd don before approaching fragile, volatile celluloid.

"I'm not shout—" He remembered then that Dupree had been present at his surprise party in the Bradbury Building. Without doubt he hadn't taken in enough paté and crackers to absorb the champagne. Valentino lowered his voice to a hush. "Talk to Kyle Broadhead. He came back from the Adriatic with a killer hangover cure."

"I talked to him. Killer's the word. Where do you even find hog thistle? You're tenth in line; and that's only because the board of regents think Broadhead's the Golden Goose and you're his fair-haired boy. Normally we assign priority according to the age of the print. Right now we're duping footage from the 1906 San Francisco earthquake."

Valentino, who had a good layman's knowledge of what went into making a new negative from an old positive, then a new master from the negative, kept his impatience to himself. "Okay. I'd appreciate a heads-up when you've started."

Dupree pressed his temples. "Don't say 'head.'"

From there Valentino went to his office in the university's old power plant, where Ruth, the gargoyle who guarded the gate, sat at her computer in the doughnut-shaped reception desk. Her long, red-lacquered nails rattled like sleet against glass as she manipulated her computer keyboard.

"Is Professor Broadhead in?"

She didn't look up from the screen. Her pulled-back, implausibly black hair and white-on-white face wore a coat of varnish as impervious as the one on her nails, and the legs of her heavy steel-rimmed bifocals hugged her temples so tight he thought they must leave grooves when she took them off. If she *ever* took them off; it was Broadhead's opinion that she slept in the building's attic, upside-down, like a bat. She was a motion-picture industry veteran whom, it was rumored, the tyrannical old studio CEOs had been too afraid of to fire. She'd occupied this particular bunker when Valentino came to work on his first day and would likely still be there when he retired in twenty or thirty years.

"If he isn't," she said, "he climbed out the window."

This reference to her alertness was no idle boast. He'd never known her to go out for lunch or take so much as a bathroom break.

He left her to continue clattering away and tapped on Broadhead's door.

"It's unlocked. I lost the key years ago."

Valentino entered just in time to see a feathered dart bury

its point in a corkboard attached to the faux-wood-paneled wall opposite the door. The board was a new feature in the Spartan office. Its concentric rings were colored individually, and numbered from five to ten, working from the outer circle to the bull's-eye. The prospect of Broadhead taking exercise of any kind was good for the front page of the faculty newsletter.

"Let me guess. Fanta's been after you to get in shape, and this is your answer."

"Don't be a loon. I address that by taking the stairs instead of the elevator the third Wednesday of each month."

"Why the third Wednesday?"

"It's the day my Social Security check is deposited. That way I never forget, and have become the fine physical specimen you see before you as a result."

The pot-bellied academic, in a corduroy jacket worn shiny at the elbows, ill-advised horizontally striped sweater vest, frayed collar, baggy slacks, and scuffed Spectators, stepped up to the board and retrieved the dart.

Valentino held his tongue as regard to his mentor's self-description; Broadhead's infamous iconoclasm did not extend to remarks directed against himself. "In that case, I can only conclude that you intend to turn this place into an Irish pub."

"English. The Irish need the extra room for drunken brawls. I can say that without incurring the wrath of HR, because my grandfather on my mother's side came from County Sligo. He disinherited Mom for marrying a Brit." He returned to his mark—it was there on the floor, an actual chalk line—and took aim.

"Where are the other darts?"

"Budget cuts." The projectile struck the target dead center. "Blast!"

"What's wrong? You hit the bull's-eye."

"Don't offer an opinion until you understand the rules. This infernal enterprise represents my work ethic."

"You call this working?"

Broadhead cocked a polished elbow toward his computer, a battleship-gray antique as big as a pizza oven. "It's how I warm up. The part of the board I hit determines the number of pages I'll write that day."

"So today it's ten."

"As on every other day, it's best two out of three. I can manage the five pages represented by the outer perimeter standing on my head—if I use fifteen-point type and three-inch margins."

"Blocked?"

"No, I just suck at darts. Blast and double-blast!" Ten again. He left the dart there and slouched behind his desk. "I can't seem to finish the damn chapter on drinking in the movies. It makes me thirsty, and I swore off liquor a year ago."

Reflecting on last night, Valentino realized he hadn't seen Broadhead do more than lift his champagne glass in salute. "Why? I've never seen you drunk."

"Nor will you. My age is the time to quit bad habits for good. That way I won't have to keep it up for long."

"So put the chapter aside and move on."

"Not an option. In addition to being a recovering alcoholic I'm an obsessive compulsive. I cannot 'move on' to Chapter Four until I've completed Chapter Three."

"You've only written three chapters? You started the book two years ago."

"Thank you for pointing that out. Something tells me you didn't come here to cause me torment. When I need that, I can always call out to Ruth."

His visitor pulled up the only other chair in the room and sat. He told him about his trip to Bozal's house and the old man's gift and what he'd asked for in return.

"You both profit," Broadhead said. "He winds up with the

director's cut of the most eagerly sought Grail in our profession, and you get yet another feather to stick in a cap that already resembles a Sioux war bonnet."

"Actually, *Bleak Street* and *Greed* are equals, in terms of being fellow victims. They were both considered to be casualties of attrition and neglect, destroyed probably to make storage room for more commercial properties."

"Like *Francis the Talking Mule.*" Broadhead stabbed a fistful of tobacco into his dilapidated pipe from the Taster's Choice can where he kept it; his disdain for the aesthetics of his vice stood shoulder-to-shoulder with his disregard for university rules and state law. He struck a match and filled the room with smoke the color of dirty cotton batting and the odor of burning tires. Valentino tipped his chair far enough back to crack the door.

"So what troubles you, sprout? Conflicted over whether to keep this latest windfall to yourself or pass it along to the university that keeps you in Milk Duds and Big Gulps?"

"No. I resolved that issue by turning it in to the lab. Maybe you can use your influence with the dean to loan it to me for the premiere. You're teacher's pet; I got that on the authority of Jack Dupree."

"And who in thunder is Jack Dupree? Sounds like a riverboat gambler."

"He's only run the lab as long as I've been here. You just gave him your hangover cure."

"Oh, yes, the black youngster with the bowling-ball dome. Did it help?"

"Never mind that. You should make an effort to learn the names of your staff."

"I'm an educator. I don't *have* a staff. That sign on my door was a gift in lieu of a raise."

"There isn't any sign on your door."

"I misplaced it along with the key. My position as head of the Film and TV Preservation Department is strictly honorary, a title to impress would-be donors in the endless round of cocktail parties I'm obliged to show up at and pretend apple juice is bourbon. I made it clear at the outset I would attend no meetings and make no decisions."

"Kind of the way you teach class."

"I never miss the first day or the last. I provide the sturdy bookends between which the teaching assistants mold young minds. Many of those moldy young minds have gone on to respectably mediocre academic careers." He took the pipe from between his teeth and let it smolder in the jar cover he used for an ashtray. "Cut to the chase, lad. Those five pages aren't going to write themselves."

"Ten."

"Speak!"

"Henry Anklemire wants me to close the case on Van Oliver's vanishing act."

Broadhead's expression was as bitter as his tobacco. "That little imp of the perverse has gotten you in Dutch more times than his closet has moths. I wouldn't complain, except sooner or later I always get sucked in."

"You always volunteered. I never asked you to do anything that would put you in danger or in trouble with the police."

"That's what I meant when I said 'sucked in.' Any muddling about in real-life crime, no matter how remote and how much dust has collected on it, is a slippery slope; and Anklemire's the banana peel. Have you ever seen even one Mack Sennett comedy in which the peel got hurt?"

"All I want is your advice."

"Tell the little troll to strap a refrigerator to his back and swim up the coast. Chances are he'll meet Oliver on the way."

"You know his heart won't be in the publicity campaign if I don't at least make the effort."

"Why ask me if your mind's made up?"

"Because I knew you'd do just what you're doing: make faces, apply a colorful metaphor in reference to Anklemire's lack of physical stature and excess of *chutzpah,* and eventually come around to give me grudging approval."

"I haven't come around."

Valentino rose, walked to the corkboard, jerked loose the dart, took up Broadhead's late position, toe to the mark, took aim, and pierced the target in the No. 5 ring.

"*Days of Wine and Roses,*" he said, dusting his palms. "The drying-out scene, with Jack Lemmon screaming in restraints. If that one doesn't kill your taste for booze, you're better off eliminating the chapter altogether."

The professor's scowl deepened. He stuck his pipe back between his teeth, drew a gnawed yellow pencil from the plain white mug on his desk, and scribbled a note on his blotter. Then he raised the pencil to make the sign of the cross. "Go with God, my son. You'll need Him."

9

AFTER HIS DEPARTMENT'S screening room, the graduate library was Valentino's favorite place on campus. Thanks in large part to Kyle Broadhead's talents at squeezing blood (donations of cash, private collections, and above all, cash), UCLA maintained an impressive, although incomplete, archive of fan magazines. It spanned the industry from the silents through Cinerama, when the voracious competition from television lured readers in droves from *Photoplay* to *TV Guide*, demolishing a publicity machine that had existed for half a century. In those pages— some slick and sturdy, others pulp and crumbling—a surprising amount of authentic Hollywood history could be found among the studio hype. It was like panning a stream for nuggets; all it required was someone who knew how to separate the genuine article from fool's gold.

Efforts to commit the material to microfilm were ongoing, but it was an expensive and tedious process, and far down the list of priorities; any major university is a honeycomb, with many bees to sustain, the drones last of all. For every draw- erful of microfilm spools, there were hundreds of periodicals moldering in stout storage cartons. These last stood in rows on steel utility shelves from floor to ceiling, like the anonymous antiquities in the government storeroom at the end of *Raiders of the Lost Ark*.

Guided by the dates in card slots (and with the help of a ten-foot stepladder), Valentino made some likely selections and carried them to a carrel and a vacant microfilm reader. Sitting, he looked forward to his chore with almost the same anticipation he brought to a screening; for him, what seemed toxic to a civilian was an adventure in time travel: Thread the film onto the pegs, switch on the glorified slide projector, crank forward, and leap ahead, days, weeks, months, years at a turn; crank backward, and enter the past. Same thing depending on which way you fanned through musty-smelling pages, the world speeding past at sixty frames a second.

There, among advertisements for Packards and Lucky Strikes, he found some production and pre-production material on *Bleak Street*. Most of it was photographic: stills of the actors in and out of costume, horsing around on the set, pretending to menace one another in tableaus similar to the scenes they'd shot. Few people studying such pictures in modern film books realized they were looking at fake publicity stills and not actual frames from the movies. By and large they were posed and shot by house photographers. Valentino, for one, sometimes wished the movies themselves looked as good as their advertising.

In our cynical time, the burlesque teasing among the players was stagy and anything but spontaneous, an attempt to show the world how well everyone got along and that even major stars didn't really take themselves seriously. In their own time, the scheme backfired, convincing outsiders that "Hollywood people" were shallow, facetious, narcissistic parasites, when in most cases they were dedicated professionals, working inhuman hours under conditions of near-slavery.

Van Oliver, it appeared, was quite chummy with Roy Fitzhugh, who played the gangster hero's bodyguard until he was killed in the first reel during an attempt on his boss's life. The pair were photographed with their arms around each other's shoulders, trading mock punches and grinning, and messing each other's Brilliantined pompadours with impudent hands. The archivist knew that such carryings-on were often a ruse to disguise deep mutual dislike, similar to the one that had led to fisticuffs between George Raft and Edward G. Robinson on the set of *Manpower*. However, there were rather more of them than the average, despite the brevity of Fitzhugh's part in the picture. Valentino was inclined to believe the two were close.

Which was a break; provided the elderly actor retained the wits necessary to remember events from so long ago. Many a promising trip to the Motion Picture Country Home had dashed itself to bits on the rocks of Alzheimer's and senile dementia. They were crueler even than the pernicious decay that had sentenced ninety percent of world film to oblivion.

Bleak Street vanished from the puff columns in June 1957— its announced month of release—as thoroughly as its star had dropped from sight weeks earlier. Under normal circumstances, the feature would have been mentioned everywhere at that time, with cover articles on its leading players in *Modern Screen* and *Liberty*, billboards splashed throughout Los Angeles and its suburbs, press kits sent out in flocks like carrier pigeons, and advertisements in newspapers in key cities across the country. Instead, the story moved to the city section of the *L.A. Times*, where burly detectives assigned to Missing Persons and Homicide were photographed grilling hapless suspects raked in from the local underworld. Almost overnight, a routine campaign intended for the Entertainment section decamped to the crime pages.

Studio clout had managed to squelch any negative publicity

concerning its chief commercial property of the season; in those "factory town" days, the police commission took its marching orders from Louis B. Mayer, Howard Hughes, Harry Cohn, Darryl Zanuck, and the Brothers Warner (none of whom realized how quickly their influence would evaporate in the face of the competition from TV). But when Hughes's people dropkicked the production, the Oliver case became open season. As his sinister background became public property, the focus of the investigation shifted from Where is he? to Where is his body? Racketeer Mickey Cohen reported to police headquarters with his attorneys, disavowing any knowledge of the missing man's fate, or for that matter the man himself: "Oh, sure, we was seen places, but I go lots of places and meet lots of people I don't remember after. I'm like the Queen that way."

"Which queen might that be?" sneered one of the reporters who'd swarmed around him on the steps of City Hall. (This from *Confidential*, the controversial scandal sheet that at the time had violated all the unspoken rules that prohibited seamy speculation.)

The obligatory sweep of known local offenders harvested a bumper crop of newspaper photos of men hiding their faces behind their hats and jut-chinned detectives subjecting pale-faced suspects to the third-degree; generations of exposure to Hollywood hype had taught the LAPD a thing or two about public relations, but the yield in solid leads was negative.

As in every successful drama, there was comic relief. A plainclothes sergeant flew to New York City to interview Mafia kingpin Frank Costello, who assured him he'd never heard of anyone named Van Oliver *or* Benny Obrilenski, and in any case Costello was a legitimate businessman, currently engaged in supplying jukeboxes to neighborhood bars. A front-page picture appeared of the sergeant emerging from a well-known brothel said to belong to Lucky Luciano, who'd been deported to Sicily for running a prostitution racket. The sergeant came home to find himself back in uniform, directing traffic at Hollywood and Vine.

The entire affair was precisely the kind of publicity the studios paid millions to avoid. The ghosts of William Desmond Taylor, a director whose murder had exposed a sordid 1920s landscape of drugs and sex, Fatty Arbuckle, a silent comic accused of involuntary manslaughter at a wild party, and sundry other figures caught up in sinful boomtown excess, had haunted the industry throughout its history, threatening it each time with stepped-up censorship and congressional investigation. No wonder *Bleak Street* was pulled and buried as deep as Oliver himself.

If he *was* buried. Once again, the "film detective" had been saddled with the unpleasant task of turning over old bones, churning up ancient secrets, and making himself equally unpopular with the people who were paid to investigate crimes and those who profited by committing them. It was like stepping from the safety of a climate-controlled auditorium onto the silver screen, and square into harm's way.

10

"TELL ME MORE about this flirting," Harriet said.

They were dining in The Brass Gimbal, a hangout that favored behind-the-scenes personnel connected to the movie industry: Foley operators, script supervisors, set decorators, wardrobe and makeup specialists, electricians, cinematographers, laboratory technicians, and sometimes second-unit directors, provided they minded their manners and weren't overheard using terms like *auteur, mise-en-scene,* or *day-for-night*; the management valued craftsmen above artists. On occasion an A-list movie star would ask for a table, but although the establishment turned away no one, a chilly reception and indifferent service discouraged a return visit.

It was far from Harriet's favorite meeting place (iceberg salad was the only item listed under "healthy choices"), but since it stood approximately halfway between the UCLA campus and LAPD headquarters, they often met there for lunch; on this day, more particularly supper. Four hours had slipped out from under Valentino unnoticed as he was convening with

Old Hollywood in the undergrad library, and Harriet was due back at work in an hour. A bus transporting prisoners from the Riverside County jail to San Quentin had gone off the Pacific Coast Highway in a fiery crash near Long Beach, claiming the lives of half a dozen convicts, and the entire CSI unit had been recruited to help out with identification.

Notwithstanding her pressing schedule, she'd taken time to change from her smock and sweats into a sleek sleeveless dress that displayed her well-developed biceps to advantage; turn over just a few more cadavers and she could out-arm-wrestle him ten times out of ten.

"Flirting, that's what you took from what I said? I'm more or less under Anklemire's orders to plunge headfirst into a sixty-year-old police case, and all you heard was a girl batted her eyes at me?"

She poked her fork at a pile of bleached pasta topped with black squid ink—the weekly Monochrome Special—like a farmer trying to skewer a trespasser hidden in a haystack. "She batted her eyes, seriously? That's the kind of detail I'm after. As for the other, you were up to your chin in disgruntled cops when we met, and many times thereafter. Who was it who said that beyond a certain point all risks are equal?"

"The captain of the *Lusitania*. She didn't exactly bat her eyes; that was just an expression. I'm not even sure she was coming on to me. Maybe she's that way with everyone and just doesn't realize what it looks like."

"You're sweet." She smiled. "And worse than blind. When you do manage to see something that isn't on cold celluloid, you talk yourself out of it."

"Are you saying you're jealous?"

"Not of you. You I trust. This girl, this Appasionetta—"

"Esperanza."

"Even worse. How do parents know? They look at one baby through the glass in the maternity ward and say, 'Esperanza.' They look at another and say, 'Harriet.'"

"You don't have to fish for compliments. You know very well you're attractive."

"Anyone can manage attractive. I want to be drop-dead gorgeous, like your Spanish *señorita*."

"I never said she was drop-dead gorgeous. I didn't even describe her."

"You didn't have to. Vixens all run to a type at that age, regardless of their nationality. My father always said if you want to know what a girl will look like in twenty years, take a look at her mother."

He put down his triple-decker burger—the BCU ("big close-up") half-eaten. His eyes had been bigger than his stomach after missing lunch, and in any case the turn the conversation had taken had squelched his hunger. "Apart from being sexist and possibly racist, there's no evidence to support it in this instance. I never met her mother, but I've seen a portrait of her grandmother in Bozal's living room. Even allowing for artistic license, she was stunning." Belatedly, he added: "Not that any other woman's looks interest me."

She laughed, instantly dispelling the gloom. "I'm teasing, Val. Any serious rivals I ever had for your affections have been dead for years. Hedy Lamarr, for example. She was brilliant *and* beautiful."

He changed his expression by force of will. He suspected he'd been pouting. "Torture isn't teasing."

"You're right, of course. It's just that it's always been a mystery to me that you never raise a fuss when I work late with those young studs in the lab."

"You dissect corpses for a living. It's not exactly soft music and candlelight." He picked up his burger. His appetite had returned. "You're just as much of a detective as the suits in Homicide. What do you make of this Van Oliver angle?"

She sat back with her Perrier (she was on duty, after all). "I'd say the danger's minimal. He's been missing since Eisenhower, and all the dese, dem, and dose guys he associated with are either six feet under or sucking oxygen from portable tanks in stir."

He stifled a smile. He couldn't imagine her using "stir" in that context before taking up with a fan of crime films and prison flicks.

She didn't notice, or feigned not to. "The police shouldn't be a problem. All the cold cases that need to be transferred to hard drive are backed up as far as the Pet Rock, so the Oliver file will go on feeding silverfish in the sub-basement at HQ through the Second Coming, or until the *L.A. Times* is hard up enough for a Sunday feature. Even if you crack the case, any egos you might bruise in the CID are on pension; worst they can do is block your parking space with their walkers."

"Oh."

"You sound disappointed."

"I was sort of hoping you'd talk me out of it. Kyle was right when he said I shouldn't have had 'film detective' printed on my business cards. I never meant it to be taken seriously."

"You should've known. Henry's been a promoter all his life. He thinks artistic license is a permit to shoot painters and po-ets." She looked at her watch, laid down her napkin, and slid out of the booth. "Gotta go see a man about some stiffs. Stay here and have dessert. The 'Key Light Pie' doesn't look too ter-ribly lethal." She stooped and kissed him on the cheek. "Give my regards to the fossils."

"I didn't tell you I'm going to the Country Home."

"You didn't have to. It's your version of Google." She breezed on out, trailing admiring male gazes all the way to the door. *Drop-dead gorgeous,* Valentino thought.

Woodland Hills, site of the Motion Picture Country Home—a facility operated by the Screen Actors Guild to keep dues-paying members in comfort and dignity during their declining years—wasn't far, but figuring in rush hour, Valentino would likely find the doors closed to visitors when he got there. He went back to The Oracle instead and did his homework.

The climate-controlled basement housed his huge store of DVDs, opposite his smaller collection of master prints in approved aluminum containers. He selected a number of titles on disc and took them up to the projection room, which doubled as his apartment. There, a laser projector mounted to the ceiling shared space with the massive twin Bell & Howells he reserved for screening movies on celluloid. He switched on the laser unit, fed a DVD into the player, and settled in for an evening filled with paranoid crooks, sadistic cops, wicked women, and lonely men pushed to the limits of human endurance.

Laura first: Murder victim Gene Tierney's portrait, haunting detective Dana Andrews from the grave; Clifton Webb's effeminate intellectual snarking his way toward double-murder; Tierney's sudden emergence from beyond the pale; and weak playboy Vincent Price, no doubt watching Webb's performance closely for future reference as his own career took a new turn shortly thereafter. The differences between the portrait that director Otto Preminger eventually chose to replace the one now in Valentino's possession were marked, but both bore a resemblance to something the film archivist could not quite place. He knew this would vex him until he found the missing link.

Double Indemnity next: Cocky insurance peddler Fred Mac-Murray, caught in the web spun by restless housewife Barbara

Stanwyck, following his male member to homicide and eventually his own death.

Pitfall. Bored suburbanite Dick Powell, derailed from marital fidelity by Lizabeth Scott's beauty and victimized innocence, threatened by the hulking jealousy of Raymond Burr (pre–Perry Mason) and cornered into the fatal shooting of another victim, a confession to the police, and the destruction of his family life.

Out of the Past. Perhaps the granddaddy of them all. Robert Mitchum refuses to send Jane Greer over for ripping off racketeer Kirk Douglas and pays for it with all three of their lives.

Each was different, but it followed a universal theme: Guilt, flight, regret, resignation, oblivion, either one's own death or the end of all that was good in his (and sometimes her) life. "Once," went the confession, "I did something wrong."

It was said these films had no color, only black, white, and gray; but he saw a deeper hue, one that blended light and shadow into a melancholy wash of fear, despair, tragedy, and regret: midnight blue. No, darker yet. Indigo.

Still in a mood to be moody (but also in the interest of laying groundwork for tomorrow), he surfed his way through a string of low-budget B-thrillers showcasing Roy Fitzhugh in brief but memorable roles, doing the hatchet work for criminal superiors, swapping one-liners with fellow fast-talking newspaper reporters, driving cabs, and ratting out his underworld colleagues. Most of these activities led him directly to his doom. From film to film he honed the dying scene to perfection, executing a mortally wounded swan dive off a rotting pier, dancing a macabre jig in step with Tommy-gun rounds slamming into his torso, smacking both palms against a pane of glass with bullets in his back. He was the Astaire of the alley, the Caruso of canaries, the Garbo of the gutter. In his best year he earned scale, the Screen Actors Guild minimum.

Valentino fell asleep during *Corpse and Robbers* and woke

up to the sound of the overture, informing him the movie had ended and the disc had returned to the menu. He switched everything off and crawled into bed without undressing.

He dozed off quickly, but heard himself saying, "Am I doing something wrong?"

II

MURDER, MY SWEET

11

HE TURNED OVER in his sleep. Something slid off his hip and struck the floor with a bang like a gunshot. He sat up straight, his heart bounding off his breastbone. He dove for the pistol under his pillow, then remembered that he wasn't one of the *noir* heroes he'd been watching all night and that he didn't own a gun.

Sunlight had found its way into the chamber, gradually dispelling his jumbled dreams and reflecting off the plastic DVD case that had fallen from the bed: Tyrone Power's cruelly handsome face with a cigarette dangling from his lip and the title, in blood-red letters gnawed around the edges: *NIGHTMARE ALLEY.*

Appropriate.

He climbed out from under the covers, spilling several more cases from the bedspread like shards of fallen plaster; wondered for a moment why he was still fully clothed, then remembered.

He was worse than an alcoholic; he was a bijou binger. Any day now he'd be checking himself into the Harrison Ford Clinic to get straight.

Harriet had given him a countertop cook stove for his last

birthday. It performed the services of both a traditional and a convection oven, a toaster, and a microwave; he wasn't quite sure, but he suspected it was a prop from a *Transformer* film. Operating it was a good deal more complicated than threading film through a projector, but he'd mastered the basics. Moving like a sleepwalker, he placed an English muffin on the toaster grate, twisted the dial, started a cup of water heating in the microwave, and opened a jar of instant coffee. He promised himself to install the usual kitchen appliances in the projection booth. His own creature comforts had taken second place behind putting the theater back on its Prohibition-era feet. It was bad enough he'd been forced to close the mezzanine men's room to the public in order to install a shower for his own use; he couldn't help feeling he'd turned his back on his customers. But he felt grungy in yesterday's clothes, and his welcome in the Bruins locker room at UCLA had long since worn out.

While he waited to eat, he retrieved his phone from a pocket and dialed a number from memory. It rang several times before Kym Trujillo answered. She sounded out of breath.

"Valentino!" she said. "Ready to check in? I can't think of anyone else your age who could hold his own in the conversation in the cafeteria."

Valentino had called the Motion Picture Country Home.

He said, "You sound like you should check in yourself. Should I call back when you're through moving furniture?"

"I wish. I just helped two nurses hoist a resident from the floor in the TV room. You know how much weight those stuntmen put on after they retire?"

"Is he all right?"

"He's fine, but the serving cart he fell on will never be the same. I'm okay, too, just a couple of cracked ribs and a ruptured spleen. Thanks for asking."

He knew this for an affectionate dig. She'd been Admissions director long enough to have faced every issue connected with caring for the elderly and egocentric, and she enjoyed her work every bit as much as he did his. "I'd like to arrange a visit with one of your residents."

"If it's the stuntman, you'll have to wait until the doc finishes pulling a twelve-piece tea service out of his belly button."

"It's Roy Fitzhugh."

Her tone warmed; her breathing had returned to normal, as he knew it would. She was five-two and ninety pounds of pure energy. "I know Roy. I admitted him myself. He's a hoot. Hang on." She came back on the line three minutes later, sounding subdued. "I talked to one of his nurses. He has his good days and his bad. Today's not so good. You might try later, after he's had his afternoon nap."

"He was sharp as a tack last time."

"Still is, if you catch him during his window."

He thanked her and said he'd call back. The exchange had sobered him. With age came wisdom, but it could steal back all it gave.

The toaster oven dinged, startling him; he'd forgotten all about breakfast. Through the glass in the microwave door, he saw that the cup of water was boiling, and for a confused second he didn't know which to address first.

The odor of burnt toast made up his mind. He tipped down the oven door, transferred the blackened English muffin to the typewriter stand he used for a dining table, fished out the steaming cup, and stirred in powdered coffee. The breadbox contained only an empty package; he'd used the last of the muffins. He scraped off the worst of the char and broke his fast crunching incinerated carbohydrates and burning his tongue with molten brew.

Not his best morning. He had a sinking feeling worse was yet to come.

He swallowed the last crumb of charcoal and let his coffee cool while he made his way by phone through a succession of robotic voices—some of them computer-generated, others just bored—arriving finally at one he recognized.

"West Hollywood Homicide, Clifford." A contralto voice, perfectly in keeping with its owner, a flame-haired, six-foot-plus Elle Macpherson type who had scorned the runway for the Los Angeles Police Department.

"Sergeant, this is Valentino. Do you remember me?"

"How could I forget? It isn't every day I crack a fifty-year-old murder case with nothing to work with but a skeleton and an amateur Columbo hopped up on Orville Redenbacher."

In that case, he thought, *you're in for a treat.*

Aloud he said, "That's getting to be a long time ago. I'm planning the grand reopening of The Oracle soon. Look for your free pass in the mail."

"Kind of you, but you didn't have to call. The mail room staff here is almost as efficient as the Criminal Intelligence Division."

"Actually, that's not the reason I called."

"Why am I not surprised?" Her tone of guarded goodwill had begun to evaporate.

It was gone entirely when he finished explaining what he wanted.

"You're worse than just in a rut; you're going backwards. The mainframe hard-drive has enough to remember without a murder investigation as old as Sputnik. The only file would be in hard copy in the bowels of City Hall, deep and dark in the center of the earth, fastened with gates and bars."

Valentino remembered his Sunday-school lessons well enough to appreciate her grasp of Biblical text. "But it *is* there?"

"Unless it went into the incinerator under LBJ. Why should I send a uniform down there to dig through the boxes with six new complaints on my desk this morning, and eight left over from last week?"

"Have someone show me where they are and I'll do the digging. It's what I'm trained for."

"There was something in *my* training about not letting civilians monkey with open cases."

"Records are public property, aren't they?"

"So file a request under Freedom of Information. You'll have it by Christmas."

"It's just research, Sergeant. I'm not looking to bring anyone to justice, even if whoever killed Van Oliver is alive and getting around on hip replacements. There's an acknowledgment in it for the LAPD when we go public. Your chief's pretty hot on shaking loose personnel to provide technical advice on movie sets; a story like this would get your PR department off *Entertainment Tonight* and on CNN."

"If you're threatening to go over my head, I've already got a permanent part there from all the traffic that came ahead of you."

"Sergeant, you know I'd never do that." But his heart was back playing handball against his ribs. The last thing he wanted to do was raise her ire.

She fell silent long enough for him to hear telephones ringing on her end, more bored voices asking for names and addresses.

"Well, I'm not letting you into the basement. I'll send a man down when I can spare him. Next week, maybe."

"If you could do it today, I'll credit you as a consultant. I'm hoping to interview a surviving witness this afternoon. I'd like to go in with all the information I can get."

The line got muffled, as if she'd cupped a hand over the mouthpiece in order to release a string of oaths. When she came back on, her tone was chilly but calm. "If you're asking me would I like to be in pictures, the answer would be 'Over my dead body,' but we don't sling that one around in Homicide. You'll get it when you get it; if you get it."

"I'll be in my office at the university till noon. Do you still have the addr—?"

He was talking to a dial tone.

12

IN HIS OFFICE, Valentino cleared a stack of old press kits, newspaper cuttings, and lobby cards from his desk and returned to a project he'd been pursuing on and off for months: trying to guess what went into a gap in the last reel of *M*, Fritz Lang's sound masterpiece; the long-missing U.S. release dubbed into English, using the standard subtitled version in an all-in-one DVD player and monitor to guide him. The first had come his way from an impound lot in Düsseldorf, where a Swiss-born cinema buff had been appointed to catalogue personal effects seized from a recently convicted Nazi war criminal.

His intercom buzzed while he was comparing Peter Lorre's impassioned plea for mercy with the original. (Disappointingly, the anonymous actor who'd provided the child-killer's voice had made no attempt to imitate Lorre's sinister inflections.) Although the ancient print had been transferred to safety stock, he switched off the Movieola to prevent the bulb from overheating and causing it damage, then answered the call.

"Cheese-it," was Ruth's only remark.

By which means he wasn't surprised to find a uniformed

officer standing outside his door. The visitor shoved a fat insulated mailer as big as a king-size pillow into his arms and stuck out a clipboard.

"You have to sign for it. Sergeant Clifford said to come back for you with the siren if you don't return it by six o'clock."

Someone had scribbled *B.O.* on the big envelope with a thick black felt-tip. The archivist, who was still stuck in Germany between the wars, took a moment to realize the initials stood for Benny Obrilenski and not body odor; although the bundle was aromatic enough. It smelled like old newspapers left to gather years of mildew in some outbuilding. He balanced it under one arm and signed the receipt with the ballpoint the officer had handed him. "Why the rush? No one's looked at it in sixty-three years."

"Buddy, you're the one that woke up the bureaucracy." The officer sneezed violently and blew his nose in a handkerchief. Valentino noticed then a smear of dust on his blue trousers, and felt a twinge of sympathy. This was the luckless grunt who'd been tagged to rummage through the heaps in some sub-sub-basement in search of this one item. He wondered what mistake the officer had made to draw such duty.

After he closed the door, Valentino rewound the German film, put it and the commercial DVD away in separate containers, and made room on the desk. The mailer was new, fastened by only a brass clasp; file material so old would be too dilapidated for safe travel without a sturdy container, and of course while it was being packed up, Clifford would make at least a perfunctory search of the contents before letting them out of her sight. She'd have made time for that, despite her workload.

The envelope was stout enough to stand upright on the floor beside his chair. He reached inside with both hands and hauled a thick sheaf up onto the desk. As it thumped down, dust billowed out in all directions. Bits of brittle rubber bands clung to the cardboard folders. Still, the files held their shape after all those years in snug confinement.

The task ahead wasn't unfamiliar. Since the dawn of Hollywood, ream upon ream of paper had accompanied each studio project: shooting scripts, inter-office memos, production notes, etc. Pawing through repositories in both hemispheres, he'd ingested enough dust, mold spores, and wood-fiber to shock a physician specializing in black lung disease. He knew enough to crack his door for ventilation, hydrate himself from time to time using the water cooler in Reception, and apply gallons of lotion to his hands to keep them from drying and cracking.

He read dozens of police reports and witness statements typewritten on yellow sheets, none of which added anything significant to his knowledge of the Van Oliver disappearance; the miasma of exasperation shared by the detectives who'd assembled them was nearly tangible. He found two photographs sandwiched between pages: a publicity shot of Oliver, smiling cautiously in a beautifully tailored suit with wide lapels, and a front-and-profile mug of Benjamin Obrilenski, not smiling, taken at the time of his arrest in Brooklyn, New York, for questioning in an election-year sweep of known or suspected offenders. On the evidence in the packet, it was the only arrest on his record, and he'd been released for lack of evidence. His physical description, printed beneath the mug, revealed he was shorter than he appeared on-screen, a mere five-foot six.

Bleak Street's director, a studio hack named Melvin Fletcher, told police he'd last seen the missing man "tying one on" at the wrap party Fletcher threw at his house on Sunset Boulevard after the end of principal photography, but didn't see him leave, and never saw him again. The officers spent considerably more time interviewing Madeleine Nash, Oliver's co-star, but she, too, claimed to have lost him in the crush at the party. She dismissed rumors of an off-screen romantic involvement with Oliver as "PR hooey." Valentino was inclined to accept this, as Bozal had told him she'd married not long after and gone to live abroad.

Roy Fitzhugh told detectives he'd accompanied Oliver out to the curb and put him in a cab that was waiting there. He'd assumed the star had called for it, as he was too drunk to drive and had declined Fitzhugh's invitation to take him home. When Oliver failed to report to RKO the next day to discuss publicity, a flunky was sent to his apartment, where he found the door unlocked and his bed made. There was no sign of disturbance, but also none to indicate he'd gone home after leaving the party.

That made Fitzhugh the last person known to have seen Van Oliver/Benny Obrilenski alive. Everyone, the host included, denied ordering the cab, and none of the local taxi companies or gypsies had any record of the fare. Consequently, Fitzhugh had been interviewed twice more, the second time at police headquarters after it was discovered he'd been detained in Mexico in 1936 on suspicion of smuggling firearms across the border from the U.S. He told detectives he'd been with his late father, a member of the Abraham Lincoln Brigade, and that the guns were intended for Republican rebels fighting in Spain. No firearms were found in their possession, and they were escorted out of the country. Roy had been only eight years old, but he could never return to Mexico.

He stuck to his story, however, and since in those turbulent days there was no shortage of Americans eager to defeat Fascism, he got the benefit of the doubt.

Clipped to this report was an eight-by-ten photo, probably from Fitzhugh's résumé, of the actor in his prime. He looked more respectable than most of his movie roles, with no cigarette-burns on his lapels or soup stains on his tie. His heavy jaw and chronic five-o'clock shadow had typecast him as mugs, lugs, and pugs in dozens of programmers; he'd shuttled from soundstage to soundstage, often without changing clothes.

Robbery was considered as a murder motive. Oliver had been paid $2,500 per week for twelve weeks of shooting, and since he had no bank account under either of his names and no cash was ever found, it was possible he had the entire $30,000—a fabulous sum then—on his person when he left the party. But the prevailing opinion, stated in memos, was that the mob, or some old rival from New York, had abducted him in a phony cab and taken him for the well-known ride. Bodies disposed of under such circumstances rarely surfaced.

Even the most high-profile criminal investigations lost steam for lack of a lead. In time the Van Oliver case slipped off the inside pages and into oblivion. For a while it would return, zombie-fashion, when feature editors ran out of material for the Sunday supplements, but eventually it was forgotten. The current generation had no patience for backstage documentaries and paperback accounts of unsolved Hollywood mysteries, leaving such fare to buffs like Valentino.

The fates of the others involved, he remembered, were varied. Madeleine Nash, *née* Magdalena Novello, quit show business, presumably for wedded bliss; Fitzhugh went on to play a one-man repertoire company of second-tier hoods, weary desk sergeants, and truck drivers until his retirement; other cast members appeared in various features, some successful, some not; director Fletcher was yanked early from his next assignment over "artistic differences" and replaced, to take his own life sometime in the early sixties when the only work he could get was directing second-unit crews for TV westerns. Valentino could only speculate what might have happened to all of them had *Bleak Street* ever seen the light of day.

He finished his coffee and called Kym Trujillo's extension. Roy Fitzhugh, she reported, was in fine fettle, having awakened fresh from his nap. He was looking forward to Valentino's visit.

13

ON HIS WAY out, he opened the door to find Kyle Broadhead standing there. The professor was holding papers.

"As much as I try to maintain a policy of never expressing gratitude—on the theory that sooner or later the party involved will require a *quid pro quo*—I've come to thank you for *Days of Wine and Roses*. Behold: five pages."

"I'm glad, but I can't claim all the credit. You should talk to Blake Edwards."

"God, no! I already owe him a favor for writing me out of *S.O.B.*" He saw the bundle under the other's arm. "Off to the bank? You may now thank *me* and we'll call it even. I'm the one who said you were wasting your time on film preservation when you're sitting on a gold mine in blackmail material."

"Nothing so felonious. I'm off to Woodland Hills, but first I have to stop by the West Hollywood police precinct and return something I borrowed from Sergeant Clifford."

"The big red dog? Good Lord, you're already in her debt for agreeing not to throw you in the hoosegow."

"I think the statute of limitations has run out on that one.

I really must be going; the brain I want to pick at the Country Home has a sell-by date."

Broadhead's face went flat. "You're doing it, aren't you? Jumping in up to your neck in another police case." He held up his hands in a defensive gesture. "Include me out. I let my membership in the Junior G-Men expire after the last time."

"What about that *quid pro quo*?"

"I knew it! What did I tell you?"

"Relax, Kyle. I'm kidding. I already owe you more than I can ever repay."

Broadhead lowered his hands. "Who are you going to see?"

"Roy Fitzhugh."

"Isn't he dead?"

"Not yet; but that's no reason to waste time." Valentino pulled his door shut. On the way to the stairs he heard Broadhead saying: "I could've sworn I went to his funeral. If I don't start making a record of these things I might wind up going to the same one over and over."

The old character actor had a cheerful room with a fine view of the Santa Monica Mountains and a TV set with a forty-eight-inch screen, where an all-female talk show clucked away in merciful silence. He wore a crisp flannel shirt buttoned to the neck, navy sweats, comfortably worn loafers, and the chirpy air of a man ready to spring out of his wheelchair and dash around the neighborhood.

Valentino did a double-take when he saw him. From Kym Trujillo's assessment of his precarious mental condition, he'd expected the man to have aged significantly since his last visit; but although he was bald except for a white fringe of hair, he was instantly recognizable from his many screen appearances.

A few wrinkles and sags did nothing to detract from his trademark bulldog jaw and bright Irish blue eyes.

"I remember you!" Fitzhugh said. "You grilled me for an hour on *Home Sweet Homicide*. Last September it was."

Valentino himself couldn't have told what month he'd visited. He wondered if Kym had been thinking of someone else when she'd expressed doubts about his mental health. "I tried to talk you into doing the commentary on the DVD. You wouldn't, so I had to pump you for everything I could get. You've brought me a great deal of happiness over the years, Mr. Fitzhugh. I've seen all your films."

"Not all."

The old man's lips pleated when he smiled. His dentures did the rest of the work, in a glass by his neatly made bed.

"Every one." Valentino looked him straight in the eye. "*Bleak Street* included."

This drew no reaction. "I got a new one opening next week at Sid's."

"Sid's?"

"Sid Grauman. I'll have him hold two tickets for you."

The founder of Grauman's Chinese Theatre had been dead for many years; and there hadn't been a new Roy Fitzhugh film since before that.

"Some screwball comedy thing," he went on. "I forget the title. Jim Stewart's in it, and that dish Kim Novak."

He understood then. Memory was a strange creature. It could leave a man shaky about things that had been said or done a few minutes previously, and razor sharp when it came to events a half-century in the past. To confuse it with the present wasn't unusual in the Home. It was the policy of the establishment to humor the victim rather than try to correct him and cause distress.

That suited Valentino's purposes down to the ground.

"You're very generous, sir. I can't wait to see it. But it's *Bleak Street* I wanted to talk about."

When Fitzhugh frowned, that famous chin bunched up like a pile of rocks. "That swish Fletcher. Said I talked through my schnozz, I should take elocution lessons. I said, 'Mr. Hughes has been paying me for a year to talk through my schnozz. If it's Ronnie Colman you want, try MGM.'"

"You were pretty friendly with Van Oliver."

"Benny's swell." For him, the production had just wrapped. "From the beginning he tells me to lay off that 'Van Oliver' stuff. He wasn't any more of a crook than my dear ol da', smuggling guns to the freedom fighters. Also he fixed it so my two scenes in the picture got scheduled on the first day of shooting and the last; that way I was on the payroll all the way through." Suddenly his eyes narrowed. "What's a college egghead want with an old dropout like me? I ain't worked since they canned me from *Barnaby Jones* for blowing my lines. That never happened before."

Valentino adjusted to the time shift. "We found a print of *Bleak Street*. The university's planning a big publicity campaign to honor the film and fund our Preservation department. Anything you could tell us about it would be a big help."

"That swish Fletcher said I talked through my schnozz. Know what I told *him*?"

He fired his next question before the conversation settled into a continuous loop. "What was Madeleine Nash like?"

Fitzhugh's face was fascinating to watch. The clouds cleared and the years fell away as if a veil had dropped.

"Maggie was a doll. She wasn't anything like the bad girl she played; that's how good an actress she was. And she had a beautiful voice: Sang old Spanish songs on the set. She was Puerto Rican, but you'd never guess it except when she sang or got tired and forgot her voice coaching. She died too young."

Valentino stiffened.

"I heard she got married and moved out of the country."

"Who we talking about?"

He'd lost him again. Time for a subject change.

"You were the last person known to have seen Van—Benny—before he vanished. Did you tell the police everything you knew?"

"Mister, they came after me with everything but a rubber hose, and they only didn't use it on account of all them reporters hanging around. You'd of thought the reason my old da' and I went down to Mexico was to raise an army to invade San Diego. Did I tell 'em everything I know!" He leaned over in his wheelchair and spat on the rug; this was the Roy Fitzhugh of *Corpse and Robbers, Cell Block, The Big Noise*: one tough gorilla with a mad-on against the world. "They'd have to beat me to jelly before I'd give 'em the time of day; then, of course, I wouldn't be able to."

That old sixth sense kicked in; the flush the film archivist felt in a bazaar in Cairo or a Culver City junk shop just before he turned and found a treasure that had sat collecting dust and no interest for years, waiting for him to come to its rescue.

He spoke carefully, afraid to startle the old man out of lucidity, yet keenly aware that he might tire at any moment and be of no use as a source of information. "Mr. Fitzhugh, do you have any idea who might have been involved in Benny Obrilenski's disappearance?"

The man in the wheelchair stared. He held this attitude so long his visitor worried that he was experiencing a seizure of some kind. He was thinking of calling for help when Fitzhugh opened his mouth. For a moment nothing came out, although he was working his lips. Then: "Talk to Ivy. If she wasn't behind it, she sure as hell knows someone who knows who was."

"Ivy?"

"Ivy Lane." A toothless grin cracked the simian jaw. "Here's where you tell me you seen all her pictures."

A plump, bouncy nurse in a floral smock knocked and entered with a blood-pressure cuff. Valentino tamped down his annoyance, ashamed at himself for resenting the Home's scrupulous attention to the residents' health. But he could hear the clock ticking. There was no telling when the window would slam shut on Roy Fitzhugh's recollections.

"One-thirty over eighty. I wish mine were as good." She undid the cuff.

"Sister, I wish more'n that." He winked and smacked her on the bottom.

Unfazed, she left them with a cheerful smile.

"Ivy Lane." Valentino jogged the actor's memory.

"Yeah. We had a name for her kind, but we didn't bandy it around like they do now. The French come up with something more polite later: *femme fatale*." He pronounced it "femmy fataly." "Could she act? Search me. What you got on-screen was what you got off it. Made Dracula's daughter look like Suzy Sunshine."

Valentino had seen her menace Cornel Wilde in *Switchback*; a statuesque ash-blonde with the ruthless beauty of a sorceress from Greek myth and the tongue of a serpent.

"But she wasn't in *Bleak Street*." He suspected Fitzhugh's mind had begun to wander again.

"Thanks to that swish Fletcher. He said I talked through my schnozz."

He leapt in before the other could return to Square One. "The director had something to do with why she wasn't in the film?"

Fitzhugh was back on track. "She was cast opposite Benny,

but Fletcher nixed her on account of she was too tall for the leading man. That was bull. It went back to *The Big Noise*, when she got Fletch fired before he'd even shot one reel. I had a bit in that one, driving a getaway car. She and him never did hit it off, and she was running around with Mr. Hughes at the time, so she got her way."

That checked. In his days as the owner of RKO, before he became a recluse, Howard Hughes had been infamous for his dalliances with his female players. "In that case, her complaint was with the director, not the star."

"You'd think. But she didn't see it that way. She thought Benny'd rigged it so he wouldn't look like a midget. She threw a hissy right there on the set; said she'd get square with Benny if it was the last thing she did. Fletcher had to threaten to call security to get her to leave."

"There must have been other witnesses. Why didn't anyone else come forward?"

"It was just us four. Benny and me was shooting close-ups to insert in post-production. Ivy just showed up, to have it out with Benny."

"What did he do?"

"Nothing. You don't know him. He never turned a hair no matter what you said or done to him. That's one of the reasons I liked him."

"Why didn't Melvin Fletcher tell all this to the police?"

Fitzhugh's face went sly. In the old days that expression had lent extra weight to his heavies. "I told you he was a swish. She called him a queer to his face during *The Big Noise*. He sure as shootin' wasn't going to come clean with the cops. It was a jailable offense, and what was worse, he'd never work in this town again."

"Still, it's a long way from there to accusing Ivy Lane of murder."

"Oh, she'd never get her hands dirty; not with her connections."

"Connections?"

Fitzhugh raised a finger and pushed his nose to one side.

"Wise guys. Back then you couldn't walk two blocks in any direction without bumping into a silk suit or one of his goons; they had the unions, the agencies, cash investments everywhere in the trade. Ivy used to date one till the spooks from the Breen office put on the pressure to break it off. I forget his name; it'd be Big Vinnie or Joey the Hippo, Little Augie Vermicelli, something anyway out of Dick Tracy. See, it was okay to *play* a bad girl, but not to be one on your own time. That don't mean she didn't stay in touch."

Valentino was seized with a double-emotion he knew well: the heady sense of having moved closer to his quest than anyone who'd gone before him, and the stark fear of what that would mean to the authorities who'd failed to make that same leap.

And the gangster angle kept coming up. No due process there, just a short trip and a sure place in Hollywood lore.

"Do you know if Ivy Lane is still alive?"

Fitzhugh stared at him, blinked. "Hitch, I didn't get those new sides. How'm I going to work if I don't know my lines?"

The actor, he'd remembered, had been cast early in Alfred Hitchcock's *The Wrong Man* before the part had gone to someone else; it was no wonder he'd never received the script changes.

The window had closed; there would be no more new revelations that day. The archivist thanked the old man for his time and left him to his past.

14

AS WAS SO often the case when it came to digging up long-ago events, the interview with Roy Fitzhugh had left Valentino with as many questions as answers.

Was Ivy Lane a murderess, if not directly, then by proxy? A spat over a casting decision seemed a flimsy motive for taking a human life; but then, the motion-picture industry was ruled by ego, and what would seem ludicrous in every other society was a matter of survival in the precarious business of entertaining a fickle public. At the time *Bleak Street* was in production, barely a generation had passed since the talkie revolution had carved a bloodbath through Hollywood royalty. The image of John Gilbert, the brightest star of his era, scraping along playing bit parts on stages he'd commanded only a few years before, was etched indelibly in memory.

William Goldman, the late great screenwriter, had said it best: "Never underestimate the insecurity of a major star."

Or:

Could the old man have deliberately misled Valentino with well-timed displays of false senility? He had by his own admission withheld crucial evidence from the police, despite the stone-age methods of interrogation in those pre–Civil Rights days. Since then he'd had decades to perfect his act. A man stuck in the unchanging routine of assisted living might exploit a young visitor's gullibility for no reason other than his own amusement.

And what of Madeleine Nash? Ignacio Bozal had provided a bucolic sketch of a gifted player who had turned her back on stardom for marriage abroad, while Fitzhugh had said she'd died "too young." How young was too young? What, precisely, did those two words mean to a man pushing ninety?

In the end, Valentino trusted neither man not to have sent him on a wild-goose chase, just because he could. Eyewitness testimony was reliable only when it was confirmed, and the Grim Reaper had swept his sickle through the population of witnesses who could corroborate or contradict their stories. When it came to cold cases, Van Oliver's was forty below zero.

He crossed the city limits and turned onto Ventura, which had been transformed into a parking lot. Police barricades blocked the lanes in both directions. Two stuntmen were fighting on the roof of a four-story building in the next block, their fists swishing an inch past each other's face, with a stack of mattresses and empty cardboard boxes reaching from the sidewalk in front to the second floor. One of the men at least would plunge into that safety net eventually.

It was a familiar disruption in L.A., but that didn't stop the natives from blowing their horns. This one would go on for a while; the camera crews on the roof and on the street were seated in canvas chairs, drinking bottled water and punching buttons on cell phones while their equipment stood idle. When the rehearsal would end and the actual filming would begin was anybody's guess, including the director's. Valentino switched off his ignition. He was nursing his domestic compact along until such time as the revenue from The Oracle laid his worst debts to rest, and the tired motor stalled whenever it idled longer than a minute.

He tapped his own horn for the sake of the brotherhood of the boulevard, then picked up his own phone and hit speed dial. One fought fire with fire, and old men with old men.

"That's never a good sign," Kyle Broadhead said.

The sign read CLOSED BY ORDER OF THE LOS ANGELES COUNTY BOARD OF HEALTH, and it was stuck to the glass entry door to The Brass Gimbal.

Valentino caught the attention of a man in a black polyester suit, white shirt, and black knitted necktie, a bureaucrat straight from central casting. He'd just finished smoothing the adhesive border to the glass.

"Is this temporary?"

"Not up to me; at least until the board sends me back for a compliance visit and I see what's what. I found a whole colony of cockroaches playing leapfrog in the salad bar."

"The Green Screen?" Broadhead said. "I *told* Fanta there's a reason rabbits don't live long."

"Where do we go now?"

Broadhead waved an arm, taking in the Starbucks on their side of the street and its double on the opposite corner. "Take your pick."

The one they chose was crowded, with a long line, but the barista in charge was efficient. Ten minutes after they entered, the pair took their tall high-dollar waxed-paper cups, a cruller, and a lemon-filled long john to one of the stand-up tables and rested their elbows. Valentino had bought, as he'd suggested the conference. While waiting in line he'd filled in his mentor on what he'd learned.

"Roy Fitzhugh," Broadhead said. "They built this town on his back. He never starred, went unbilled often as not; just showed up on time every day, sober and on his mark, lines down pat, and made ten pictures to Clark Gable's one. No Oscars, not even a nomination, but he lent money to some who won."

Valentino blew steam off his cup. "I didn't realize you knew so much about him."

"I don't; yet I do. He represents an endangered species. Movies are technically better than ever, and their top-notch talent are almost worth their confiscatory salaries, but the industry will never again have the deep bench of supporting players it had in the old days. As soon as one gets more than a just a mention in the trades, the studio builds a feature around him, and lets whatever other project that might have benefited from his contribution collapse under its own weight. And so Adam Sandler winds up carrying the film on his hydrocephalic head."

"Stirring speech, Kyle, although if you're planning to address a Guild meeting you'd better be sure Happy Gilmore isn't in attendance."

"I don't give speeches; it's in my contract. I'm quoting chapter two of the new book."

"I'll be sure and pick up a copy. Right now it doesn't solve my dilemma."

"It's not *your* dilemma. Go back to Henry Anklemire and tell him he'll have to work with what he's got. He'll whine a spell and kick a cat out a window, then put his nose to the stone." He shook his head. "All this time you've spent around old crocks like me and you still haven't learned you don't have to do anything you don't want to."

"I do if I want to keep on paying my bills."

Broadhead dunked his pastry in his coffee and twirled it like a swizzle. "They call me an ornament of the university. You know what an ornament is? A strip of colored paper you throw out after a party. It's the pillars that stick."

"I'm a pillar?"

"Shut up. I don't know why the sky pilots call pride a sin. Modesty's worse. Every time you snag a rare film and give it to the program, you dig your toe in the dirt and say your reward is in serving the cause of cinema history. You've accomplished more than all your predecessors put together."

"I wouldn't say—"

"Sinner! Damn it, man, you need to cash in on your reputation! You could strangle the dean's wife live on TMZ and he'd have Anklemire spin it so it came out you were giving her the Heimlich maneuver. You're bullet-proof, and you're afraid a Nerf ball will shatter a rib."

Valentino watched him rescue the sodden doughnut from ruin. It seemed to require all his concentration. "I guess I could just walk away."

"You *guess*? Were you this clueless when I had you in my class, or am I the only one here who's getting smarter?"

He let Broadhead have that one. It was preferable to the reaction he'd get if he told him he didn't *want* to walk away. He had the scent now.

He took a last bite of his cruller and a swig of coffee. It was still hot enough to poach an egg. "Let's blow."

Broadhead stared. "How many of those hard-boiled flicks have you been watching?"

They bussed their table and stepped outside. The sun had dipped below the smog, tinting its normally brown underside an eerie shade of copper. Like the green sky that warned the Midwest of a tornado, it promised a major ozone alert by morning, and with it the standard official admonition to avoid going outside, which few locals obeyed. Valentino was parked across the street. He offered Broadhead a lift.

"I'll walk. It may be my last fresh air for a spell. Also I enjoy the look on the faces of Angelinos when they see a man using his feet for something other than the gas pedal."

They shook hands and the archivist stepped off the curb.

"Look out!"

A black, slab-sided town car with shuttered headlights sped straight at Valentino. He leapt back onto the sidewalk just as it swept past, close enough to snag the hem of his jacket in the slipstream. Braking, its tires shrilled, slewing the vehicle into the curb.

The window hummed down on the passenger's side and the driver leaned across the seat, framing his face in the opening. Teak-colored eyes in a nut-brown face caught Valentino's gaze. "Sorry, buddy. Didn't see you. I will next time."

The car slammed into gear and was gone around the corner before Valentino could react.

Broadhead seized him by the shoulders from behind and spun him around. "That maniac! Are you okay?"

"Did you hear what he said?"

"No. What?"

Somehow it sounded even more suggestive when he repeated it.

"Huh." The professor looked at the little haze of dust still settling in the car's wake. "I guess this would have been a good time to get a license number."

15

"DO YOU THINK I should report what happened to the police?"

In the passenger's seat, Broadhead frowned at the windshield. After the close call with the town car he'd changed his mind about walking back to the office. "I can't advise you there. You're the one who almost wound up a hood ornament."

"It could have been an accident. What did the man say that was really suspicious?"

"You're right. This old-time mob angle is turning us into nervous Nellies."

"On the other hand, what does 'I won't next time' mean? What's the population of L.A., anyway?"

"Three and a half million, give or take a dress extra."

"So what are the odds there'll be a next time?"

"Good point. It was a veiled threat."

"But if it was deliberate, he could have clipped me anyway. All he had to do was bump up over the curb. I've done that by accident, turning a sharp corner."

"Me, too. He was just shook up and said the first thing that came to mind."

"Still, the way he said it. In a monotone, like a hoodlum in a B movie."

"Now that you mention it. Better report it."

"They'd laugh me out of the station, and they'd be right. These things happen a hundred times a day. Nobody in southern California goes anywhere except on wheels, and the speed limit's a joke."

"Yup. Just forget it."

"Thanks, Kyle. Talking with you always clears my head."

"What I'm here for."

Dusk wasn't just gathering; it was coming in on the gallop. The shadows cast by the Sierras pushed hard toward the Valley under a low ceiling built of coastal fog and auto exhaust. Homeward-bound traffic clogged every major artery and most of the minors, but Valentino swam against the current. He dropped Broadhead off to collect his own car and went back to his office in the old power plant, to return the dubbed *M* to the secure storage vault next to the lab and to think about his next move.

He hadn't been fooled by Kyle's performance in the car. The wily old lecturer had used that Socratic ploy hundreds of times in his class, leading a skeptical student around in tight circles until he came to reject his own pet theory as ludicrous. In this case, the object had been both to prevent Valentino from paralyzing himself with panic and to keep him on his guard. How often had the old pedagogue said it? "Just because you're paranoid doesn't mean someone isn't out to get you." The trick was to shelve one's fear until he could confirm the reason for it and act on what he'd learned.

However, Valentino had withheld something from his mentor that might have changed the object of the lesson; had Broadhead seen *Bleak Street*, he might have noticed what he had.

He'd glimpsed the face in the open car window for less than two seconds, but everything about it—the shape, the coloring, the set of the features—bore so close a resemblance to the young Van Oliver that he might have been his double.

Of course, it was just fantasy, fueled by shock; which was why he hadn't bothered to share the observation. A crime from the past, a dangerous woman, and now a seeming resurrection from the grave: This whole adventure was veering too close to the plot of a *noir* film to be anything but illusion.

Ruth, a fixture as always, looked up from the memorandum on her desk; she was crossing out entire passages in red pencil, like a teacher grading a term paper. It might have been written by Broadhead or anyone else in the department who shared her services. Nobody connected had ever summoned up the courage to challenge her right to edit their communications. She pointed the stiletto blade of her pencil toward the door of his office.

"Visitor."

"And you just let him in?"

"This is a public-funded institution of learning, not Area Fifty-one. Do you think anyone could smuggle so much as a stolen paper clip past me? Also it isn't a him." She stuck out a business card.

He took it. An impressionistic pen-and-ink sketch in the corner limned a gaunt vulpine torso and face with baleful eyes, brows that soared like raven's wings, and neon-red lips: Theda Bara, silent star of *Cleopatra* and many other man-eating roles during the early silent period (all gone now, an entire career lost to attrition and neglect): the first *femme fatale*. She was touted as the daughter of a Middle Eastern potentate, her name an anagram of "Arab Death." In truth she'd been born Theodosia Goodman in Ohio. The Hollywood propaganda machine hit the ground running as early as 1917.

To the right of the drawing and below, engraved in shiny black letters, was a legend, followed by several contact numbers:

TEDDIE GOODMAN
CHIEF CONSULTANT
SUPERNOVA INTERNATIONAL

No, it wasn't the legendary Theda, although in person it was an easy assumption. Valentino suspected the name was an alias, adopted to catch the eye of her employer, Mark David Turkus, billionaire founder of Supernova, UCLA's fiercest competitor in the business of locating, restoring, preserving, and marketing lost cinematic treasures. Valentino suspected further that she'd taken the idea from his own name, coincidentally the same as another legendary silent star's. He could prove his identity from his birth certificate, but not having seen hers, he could only speculate based on her long record of manipulation and underhanded practices. She could give lessons to Theda's predatory dames in the arts of bribery, subterfuge, and seduction.

"Teddie," he greeted, pulling his office door shut behind him. "How nice of you to show up without the bother of a satanic rite."

She was sitting behind his desk, her pencil arms spread and her white hands braced palms down on the top, forming an indestructible triangle. Today she had on a sleeveless dress of some shimmering green metallic material that fit her as tightly as the skin of a snake; it looked as if she'd need a can opener to get out of it. She wore her enameled black hair smoothed straight back from her high pale forehead, and her jet-trail eyebrows drew a *V* (for vampire) above a long straight nose and scarlet slash of mouth.

"Not funny," she said.

"Not meant to be." He hiked a hip onto the corner of the

desk and rested a hand on his thigh. It was never bad policy to affect a casual attitude in her presence. The room temperature always seemed to drop ten degrees when she walked in. "It's been a while. The Augustine murder case, wasn't it?"

"As you know full well. If it hadn't been for me, there'd be four fresh plots in Forest Lawn. While the rest of you eggheads were running this way and that, splicing useless clues like it was one of your precious movies, I got the drop on the worst mass-killer in this state since Charles Manson." Films to her were commodities only.

"No argument; but what have you done lately?"

Twin streaks of crimson appeared on the polished-pearl skin that covered her cheekbones, to fade as quickly as desert blossoms after a rain. Teddie Goodman's goat could be gotten, but never for long. She pointed a bare shoulder at the file cabinet where he'd stashed *M*. "Congratulations. Where's the rest of it?"

"Someplace with a better lock. Seems to me the last time you went snooping among my stuff, a couple of apes threw you down a flight of stairs. Most predators learn from their mistakes."

"Mark wanted to take you to court for that. You know he'd win; even if the university stood behind you, he'd have buried it under a pile of Tiffany-class lawyers. I told him if he did that, you'd just get fired. It'd take us a week to find out who replaced you and a month to figure out his working method, whereas with you still on the job all I had to do was follow you around until I found out what you were after, then sprint past you to the finish. He'd seen me do it often enough."

"I tripped you up a couple of times," he said. "Anyway, what's past is past. What's brought you slumming around the halls of academe this time?"

"How far are you along on putting *Bleak Street* into circulation?"

He slid off the desk, to avoid falling, and cleared a heap of yellowed press releases off the other chair in the office in order to sit down. This gave him time to recover. "Who's your pipeline into the LAPD?" There was no use denying anything where Teddie was concerned. She never struck until she was sure of her information.

"What makes you think I have one?"

"Only a few people know I have anything to do with the film. I'm sure of the ones I've known for years, and the most recent is an unlikely informant based on his health and living arrangements. That leaves the police, who I asked for the files on the Van Oliver disappearance. They run a tight ship, but it's been known to spring leaks."

Her expression didn't change; but then it would take a jack-hammer to crack her features. "If you repeat that in front of witnesses, I'll sue you for slander. Any tank-town shyster could win that one. I asked you a question."

"Give it up, Teddie. It's a donation, acquired legally by its former owner, and it's in a secure facility even your high-tech skeleton keys can't crack. Tell the Turk he's barking up the wrong tree this time."

"How it was acquired remains to be seen; but it wouldn't matter."

"And why is that?"

"Because possession and ownership are two different things when it comes to intellectual property. Say you have a letter addressed personally to you by Brad Pitt. You can sell that letter to someone else, but you can't publish its contents without the permission of the copyright owner; Brad Pitt, in this hypothesis. You can't release *Bleak Street* for public viewing and charge a fee unless the owner of the copyright agrees."

"RKO ceased to exist sixty years ago. Who could the owner be?" But he had the sinking sensation that he knew the answer.

When Teddie Goodman smiled, he could hear the hissing of a fuse. "Must I say it?"

He didn't reply.

She rolled a polished shoulder. "Supernova International bought out the entire RKO library last month, as well as all properties belonging to the studio's successors, Desilu and Lorimar: Everything from *Cimarron* to 'Who shot J.R.?' The minute you open *Bleak Street* anywhere, you and your employers will be up to your neck in subpoenas. But I like you, Valentino, and so does Mark. We have no interest in exposing you to public humiliation."

From her lap she drew a clutch purse made of glistening black leather trimmed with the same metallic green fabric as her dress and opened the clasp. It was just large enough to contain the No. 10 envelope she placed on Valentino's side of the desk. This bore the embossed return address of the District Court of the County of Los Angeles.

"This is a judicial order restraining you from engaging in any public exhibition of the property known as *Bleak Street* until such time as you can show cause in court how such exhibition would not infringe upon the rights of the owner of the said intellectual property. The formal language is more involved, but I'll leave the whereases and hereinafters for you to work out in private." She snapped the purse shut.

Valentino didn't pick up the envelope. "You're devious, but I've never known you to lie. If you say that's what this is, I'm sure it's genuine."

"I like you too."

"Hear me out. With us in possession of the film and Supernova in control of the copyright, I'm sure we can work out a deal that's beneficial to us both. There might even be a substantial corporate tax benefit involved. I'm sure Mr. Turkus' attorneys will be able to work out the details."

She pursed her lips, collapsing her cheeks so that they appeared even more cadaverous than usual.

"We can come to a deal, but I doubt you'd like it."

"I'm listening." He braced himself. He knew this was going to be bad. Later he would have to admit that he never dreamed just *how* bad.

"It's my employer's intention," she said, "to see that *Bleak Street* is never released. In order to guarantee that, he's prepared to invest as much of his resources as are necessary to buy all existing prints and negatives of the property and then destroy them."

Valentino stared. Her face gave no indication that she was joking. In fact he knew from long association that Teddie Goodman was incapable of either expressing humor or appreciating it.

She smiled for the second time in one visit, breaking a precedent. "I forgot to congratulate you on The Oracle's grand opening. How soon can Mark and I buy tickets?"

16

AFTER SHE LEFT, Valentino called Smith Oldfield with the university's legal department and made an appointment for the next morning. Then he went home, turned off his cell, and unplugged his landline. His sleep was uninterrupted, but he dreamed of close encounters with speeding automobiles, cunning old men with pliant memories, and slinky vamps luring callow young men silently to their doom.

In the morning, Oldfield, ever the gentleman, opened the door of his office personally to admit him. The New England–born attorney, who traced his ancestors back to the *Mayflower* (not that he was ever crass enough to mention it), rarely kept anyone waiting for long.

The office might have been constructed in Boston and transported across the country to a soundstage, all ready for Lewis Stone or Sidney Blackmer or Louis Calhern to cloud the air inside with phrases like *habeas corpus, amicus curiae, voire dire,* and *actus reus*; terminology that Kyle Broadhead liked to dismiss as "body-snatching from linguistic graveyards, sanctioned

under the law." It was all leather and oak, cream-colored bind-
ings, fox hunts and diplomas.

The lawyer, tailored comfortably in well-seasoned wool,
stepped to a paneled cabinet. "Coffee? I promise I can improve
upon the supermarket blend they serve in the break rooms."
He swung open a cabinet containing a black-and-silver Keurig
coffeemaker and something else that caught the visitor's eye:
a sleek gold statuette a little over a foot tall, with what looked
like a strip of black electrical tape masking the engraving on
its base. Oldfield took the appliance out quickly and swung the
door shut.

"Was that an Oscar?"

The attorney placed the Keurig on a credenza and plugged it
in, taking more care than seemed necessary for the operation.
"I'd rather you hadn't seen that. My office cleaner failed to put
it back in its proper place. I can't tell you whose name is on it."

"I didn't think it was yours. I doubt the bar association would
look kindly on a lawyer winning an award for acting."

"I performed a service for a friend. I told him he didn't owe
me anything, but he insisted I hold the, er, item until he can
pay me for my time and expenses."

"Do you think he will?"

"Yes. And not just because he wants to put that thing back
on his mantel."

"May I ask how long it's been?"

Oldfield's face was a blank wall. "He'll be back for it."

There was no use pursuing the subject. This particular officer
of the court would carry a confidence to the grave.

Valentino declined coffee with thanks. Oldfield looked disappointed; clearly he was proud of his brew, and the other regretted
his decision. They repaired to a cluster of deep club chairs and
sat down facing each other. Everything about the host, from his

crisp gray temples to the shell-rim glasses he held in his lap, suggested that he'd made the transcontinental trip along with the smoky Ivy League furnishings.

Valentino knew all this for set-dressing. Oldfield was as thoroughly grounded in show-business psychology as anyone else in town. The opposing counsel who on first impression expected him to enter the ring with reticence, reserve, and old-school decorum was quickly disillusioned. He was a tiger in tweed.

"How *is* Miss Goodman?" he said, once the nature of Valentino's business was explained. "She should have recovered from her injuries by now. I envy you young people your resiliency."

"She's resilient; some might say she's positively reptilian. She grows a new limb for every one lost." Valentino handed him the court order.

Oldfield donned his readers and unfolded the stapled-together sheets. He read them with close attention, as if he were alone in the room. For all his genteel manners, when it came to the nuts and bolts of his profession, he made no concessions to cheery optimism: His clients were left to draw what they might from his "Hms" and head-shakes. To all appearances, were he a physician studying a patient's chart, he was preparing to deliver a fatal diagnosis.

Finally he refolded the papers and his glasses. Cleared his throat. Valentino prevented himself from leaning forward only with effort.

"I'm afraid it's more than a nuisance suit," Oldfield said.

"That comes as no surprise. A five-car pileup on the freeway is a nuisance. Teddie's a natural disaster."

"Hm. If Supernova is indeed in sole ownership of the RKO library—and based on what I know of the judge who signed it, I cannot imagine anything has been overlooked—the corporation is within its rights to enjoin you from exhibiting the property in question. To do so would constitute an assumption of ownership."

"But I do own it. Or rather, UCLA does now."

"In a case involving intellectual property, to possess is not to own."

"Can we fight this?"

"One can *always* fight; that's the spirit behind the rule of law. The *letter* is something else again. I could not counsel pursuing the matter with any assurance that the result would not be as it stands at present."

Valentino nodded. He felt as if he'd been given a straight answer to the question, "How long have I got?" He rose and held out his hand for the papers. "Thank you, Mr. Oldfield."

"Perhaps you could meet with Mr. Turkus and come to some kind of terms outside the legal arena."

"Doubtful. Teddie made it clear he intends to prevent the film from ever being shown to anyone, anywhere, under any circumstances."

"That seems extreme."

"I can't fathom it myself. Our entire history has been one of us determined to beat the other to a property and then bringing it out in the public arena. This new wrinkle has me scratching my head."

"To put it mildly." The lawyer gave him back the court order. His expression was illegible. Years of experience with judges and juries had gone into the construction of that poker face. "It's none of my business, I suppose; but assuming you'll take my advice and avoid going to court, may I ask what you intend to do?"

Valentino hesitated. "If I answered that question, could I be assured it won't leave this room?"

Oldfield frowned. "Client confidentiality doesn't extend to

committing an illegal act before it takes place. I cannot withhold prior knowledge of a crime."

"Thank you, Counselor." Valentino shook his hand again and
let himself back out into a morning that anywhere but in southern California would pass as twilight.

17

"VALENTINO?" SAID THE woman on the other end of the telephone.

"Valentino," said Valentino.

"Seriously?"

"Unfortunately."

She chuckled. The distinctive husky voice had been further roughened by sixty years of cigarettes and aging vocal cords. "I was told you died seven years before I was born."

"I'm glad I didn't. I'm a fan."

"You needn't flatter me, Mr. Valentino, or whatever your real name is. What can you want of an old relic like me?"

Ivy Lane had proved remarkably easy to locate. Decades after her last appearance on film—one scene in an episode of *Ironside*—she was still a paid-up member of the Screen Actors Guild, where a contact had passed along her address and phone number, swearing him to strictest confidence.

He'd decided to play it straight. To one of his temperament, laying his cards on the table came more easily than subterfuge, and usually led to better results.

"I'm with the Film and TV Preservation Department at UCLA. I'd like to interview you about your involvement with the filming of *Bleak Street.*" He held his breath. If his interest made her suspicious enough to refuse, it would at least indicate that Roy Fitzhugh hadn't made up the story of a confrontation on the set.

Did he hear a slight gasp? It was difficult to tell over the wire. When she spoke, her tone was unchanged.

"Great heavens. I haven't heard about that one in many, many years. I'm sorry to disappoint you, but I *had* no involvement in the production. I had to leave the cast because of a scheduling conflict."

He fudged a bit (but then so had she, if what Fitzhugh had said was on the level). "That was my information. It's what I wanted to ask you about."

"It's a filthy day. Would one o'clock tomorrow be convenient?"

He hesitated, then said it would be if it was for her, and they broke the connection.

Her invitation, coming so quickly, had been unexpected; but if this turned out to be another bum steer, he'd at least have the pleasure of adding another personal meeting with a silver-screen icon to his collection.

Valentino had no idea why Teddie and Turkus wanted to suppress *Bleak Street*; but he was just as determined to crack the Van Oliver case. He could no more stop what he'd started than he could throw a projector into reverse in the middle of a showing, breaking the film beyond repair.

The scenery outside the power plant was depressing. The smog lay now on the rooftops, causing school closures and warnings to the elderly and the very young to remain indoors. There was an advantage to Valentino that the dip in senior-citizen shuttles and school buses made the rush hour less harrowing than usual. He reached Santa Monica in record time. There a retired Foley mixer had promised him a lead to the missing courtship scene from the Judy Garland/James Mason *A Star Is Born*; for years, restorers had been forced to use production stills to bridge the plot gap under the existing soundtrack. The film's popularity suffered: Moving pictures were expected to move. But once he got there, the old man tried to hold him up for a bribe in return for information that was patently a bluff.

"Thanks for your time," he said, turning toward the door; *and for wasting mine.*

He was disappointed, but not devastated. Most leads led nowhere, through deliberate misdirection or faulty memory or mistaken notions of the worth of the item in play; it was part of the game, and one reason that a true discovery tasted so sweet. On this smutty day, however, the return trip stuck him in the slow-moving sludge of hometown traffic, with nothing to entertain him on his AM-S/M radio but gas-bag talk show hosts, a college basketball contest for dead-last in the standings, ads pitching cures for erectile dysfunction, and rap marathons that left him with a pounding headache and despair for the future of the human race.

"'The Man that Got Away' my foot, Judy," he said aloud. "Make that my career."

"No one said it'd be all gala premieres and your footprints on the Walk of Fame, Val."

This voice, the only other one in the car, made him jerk the wheel. The driver of a Land Rover passing him on the right blasted his horn, sending him back over the line.

He wrestled his cell phone from his pants pocket and glanced at the screen. He'd butt-dialed Kyle Broadhead, who'd overheard every word. Valentino hit END without replying.

———

Overnight the wind shifted to the southwest, blowing the noxious clouds out over the Pacific. A freshly minted sun in a clear sky shone on pink stucco, yellow adobe, red ceramic tile, and swimming pools like bits of sparkling blue glass. It was one of those mornings the Chamber of Commerce chose to roust photographers from bed in order to take the postcard shot for the tourists. With no pressing issues awaiting him at work, Valentino took his toasted bagel and fresh-squeezed orange juice out onto the rear terrace to read the trades and spend the morning admiring Max Fink's neighborhood: the place as it had looked in 1927, when the box-office baron broke ground on The Oracle.

Afterward, its new owner put on a pale blue shirt and his best summerweight suit. He debated with himself over whether to wear a necktie, then selected one of the handful he kept for excursions east. The old Hollywood and the new had different standards. He wanted to make a good impression.

Driving, he split his attention between the rearview mirror and the road, looking for black town cars with shuttered headlights. When none materialized, he relaxed. A steady diet of crime movies was bad for the imagination.

He drove among convertibles with their tops down, waving at clever-faced youths selling maps to the stars' homes (the scuttlebutt they sometimes sold him was a good deal more reliable than the maps themselves, dozens of which crammed his glove compartment with their out-of-date information), entered Laurel Canyon, and pulled into a scooped-out parking area at the base of a stupendously long flight of flagstone steps. His watch read 12:45 P.M. He hoped he wouldn't be late; he hadn't counted on having to scale the Matterhorn.

The house was one of those stately sprawling old Spanish villas pegged to the side of the canyon, a fortunate survivor of the wildfires that visited the place almost annually. Heavy rain in the spring created lush undergrowth, to be turned into kindling when the Santa Ana winds blew hot and dry from Mexico; all that was required was a spark from a backyard grill or a carelessly flung cigarette butt or just a heated argument to turn the place into an inferno. (Broadhead: "Fires, hurricanes, mudslides, earthquakes. God threw us out of Paradise once. When will we get the message?")

The steps staggered up and up and up the geological ages, literally a stairway to the stars: When Beverly Hills ran out of room for private palaces, the glitterati had fled this direction. Climbing with the aid of an iron handrail, Valentino felt a niggling sense of *déjà vu*. He wondered where he'd seen the place before. He was sure this was a part of the canyon he'd never visited.

Then he remembered: It was the house where Ivy Lane had shot Cornel Wilde in *Switchback*. These were the very steps where Wilde had stumbled and then rolled down, tumbling end over end, bouncing off stone and iron, finally landing on his back in the street. Blank, staring eyes turned toward a heaven too far beyond his mortal reach, captured in extreme close-up as sirens approached, growing louder and louder until THE END came up and the orchestra drowned them out.

Fade to black.

Co-star Ivy Lane had either lent her own home to the production or formed some kind of attachment to it during filming and bought or rented it later; years later, perhaps, in a fit of nostalgia. It looked less forbidding, almost cheerful, in color on a sunny day than it had in black-and-white. Someone had removed the sinister hedges and planted flowers in boxes under the windows.

Had he come there after dark, when the jagged stone steps and the pale-stucco house at the top would be lit only by the streetlamps strung out along the base of the cliff, leaving the rest in indigo shadow, he might have made the connection immediately. As it was, he had the eerie sensation of having stepped directly into a frame from a motion picture.

The house itself was typical of the regional culture, an *hommage* to the haciendas that had been brutally bulldozed to make room for an earlier generation of bungalows and motor courts. On the expansive front porch, Valentino leaned against a post of piñon pine and waited for his breath to catch up and his heart rate to slow to normal. It had been a long ascent even for a young man, and part of it through Cornel Wilde's ghost. Finally he pushed away from the post, straightened his tie, and pressed a coral button in a verdigris copper setting.

Instantly the door was opened by a man whose broad bulk filled the opening as thoroughly as a second door. Valentino had the uneasy feeling that he'd been tracked all the way from the floor of the canyon, like an intruder wandering into an ambush. The man wore a tan poplin sportcoat over a white tailored shirt, open at the neck to display his smooth tanned muscular throat. His hair started two inches above the bridge of his flat nose and grew so close to the skull it left the bony structure exposed. Black, tiny eyes under a rocky outcrop of brow and a blue-coal chin suggested a direct line to Cro-Magnon man. In Ivy Lane's day, he'd have been the man who stood behind the man barking the orders, wearing tight-fitting chalk stripes and a white tie on a black shirt.

The first words out of the man's mouth were even less encouraging than his monolithic demeanor.

"Are you with the police or the coroner's office?"

18

THE VOICE WAS a deep drum roll. Stepping back, Valentino stared up into a pair of nostrils like ship's funnels. The line he'd been fed (he thought it a tasteless joke) sounded rehearsed; once again he had that sense of Been There Before. He knew this man from somewhere.

"Neither," he said. "I have an appointment with Miss Lane. The name is Valentino."

The man-mountain rumbled. The noise seemed to indicate amusement. "Yeah, sure."

He suppressed a sigh. Establishing his right to a name so well known in the entertainment world presented an obstacle almost daily. One generation remembered the star of *The Sheik* and *Blood and Sand*, avatars of the silent era; another compared him to a fashion designer of international renown. So far as he knew, he was related to neither. Experience had taught him to keep his business cards handy. He gave one to the ogre, who glanced at it and poked it into his handkerchief pocket.

"All her appointments are canceled, sorry." The door started to close.

A female voice called from the other side of the poplin sport-coat. "Who is it, Vivien?"

Vivien?

"Someone who says his name is Valentino. He has cards." He sneered the last sentence. "I told him—"

"Yes, I heard that part. Show him in."

When at last the giant stirred, it was like tectonic plates shifting. He moved to one side, leaving just enough space for Valentino to enter the house sideways. Coming from bright sunlight, he was blinded temporarily by the dim illumination inside. From out of the gloom came a hand, trapping his in a solid grip. As his pupils caught up, he found himself facing a woman nearly as tall as he. She wore large red-framed glasses and a tailored red suit without a blouse. This did wondrous things for a figure that didn't seem to need to have much for it. Her honey-colored hair was caught loosely behind her neck.

"I'm Georgia Tanner, Miss Lane's legal representative. She mentioned your conversation."

"Then I won't have to explain myself."

"Something about one of her films."

"*Bleak Street*; except it really wasn't one of her films. She dropped out before the cameras rolled."

"What business are you in again?"

Vivien retrieved the card from his pocket, looked at it again, and presented it.

"'Valentino,'" he said, as if she couldn't read what was on the card. "'Film Detective.' A dick. I said it the second I saw him."

Looking at him again, Valentino felt a shock of recognition. Now that there was some distance between them, he could take in the huge man's blunt features and heavily muscled build in perspective. He was older than he looked; splinters of silver in his stubble suggested he dyed his hair. In the early eighties, under the name "Bull" Broderick, he'd been interviewed in *TV*

Guide as Lou Ferrigno's stunt double in *The Incredible Hulk*. The foyers and pantries of Greater Los Angeles were littered with more half-forgotten faces than a cutting room floor.

Valentino told Georgia Tanner where he worked. "Calling myself a detective gets more attention in the entertainment industry than archivist. My job is to locate and acquire rare motion pictures so they can be preserved for future generations to see and appreciate."

"Goodness, you *are* a detective."

"In a way. Some films seem just as determined to stay lost as any fugitive from justice." He was suffocating from the lack of a change of subject. "May I see Miss Lane?"

"I don't see what help she could be, since as you say she wasn't in—what was it, again?"

He repeated the title. He was pretty sure she hadn't forgotten it. At this point in her career, she had yet to develop Smith Oldfield's impervious mien. "So far as I know, she's one of only two surviving actors who had anything to do with the production. Forgive me, but I didn't think I'd have to jump through hoops just to ask your client some friendly questions."

The professional smile left her face. "Miss Lane is dead. She committed suicide late last night or early this morning."

The news came as a physical blow. He was struck by the thought that he'd never lived in a world that didn't contain Ivy Lane. She had sounded so lively over the phone, so much more like herself than the dozens of starlets who had attempted to imitate her in roles patterned after her iconic image.

"Have the police definitely established suicide?"

"We're waiting for them now," Georgia Tanner said. "She always came down promptly at eleven for lunch. Today, when she was more than a half hour late, Vivien went up to look in on her. He tried to wake her, but her skin was already cool. He called me at my office and I came straight over. I found an empty prescription bottle on her bedside table. It was Seconal."

"Vivien is the butler?"

"Bodyguard," said the giant.

Valentino looked from him to the attorney. "Why would an eighty-seven-year-old woman need a bodyguard?"

"She didn't. She hadn't since she quit being Hollywood's Bitch Goddess when Cinemascope came in." She smiled tightly. "Does my language shock you?"

"I'm familiar with all the euphemisms: femme fatale, bad girl, vamp, harpy, bitch goddess. They predate the rating system."

"Yes." She seemed disappointed. "Anyway, she was accustomed to having one around. She played so many spider women, you see, and some moviegoers in those innocent days had trouble separating the image from the reality. That was over long before Vivien came. In his ten years here he's been more of a companion. He was absolutely devoted to her."

"Still am."

Did the big man's voice break? Valentino looked at him again. His eyes were pink around the edges and slightly swollen. He felt a little more kindly to him then. They were both fans of Ivy Lane.

"Can either of you think of a reason she'd want to end her life?"

A glance passed between attorney and bodyguard. She shook her head. "That's up to the police, I suppose."

"May I see her?"

She was startled. "Whatever for?"

"I've only known her on-screen. This may be my last chance to see her in—well, person."

"Creep." Vivien spoke under his breath.

Georgia Tanner consulted the floor. It was blue and white Mexican tile, the same shining squares William Demarest had dropped his cigar ashes on when he came to investigate the armored-car robbery at the center of *Switchback*'s convoluted plot.

She looked up. "I don't suppose it would do any harm, if you don't touch anything."

"I go too." It was a line Vivien never got to use in his non-speaking *Hulk* role.

They passed through large, sun-splashed rooms and up an open swirl of staircase with a brass banister like the railing of an ocean liner. Original paintings for posters advertising Ivy Lane's movies lined the staircase wall: Ivy locked in steamy embraces with Wilde, Dick Powell, John Payne, Robert Mitchum, Alan Ladd. Invariably, a shadowy figure lurked in the keylit background, gripping a gun; Peter Lorre, Elisha Cook, Jr., Steve Brodie—a pictorial *Who's Who* of heavies from Central Casting's exhaustive inventory. One of the great Dark Ladies of the uncertain postwar period, Lane was the stereotypical seductress who lured the ambivalent hero to the wrong side of the law, and eventually his doom—and hers as well, as dictated by the code laid down by the censorship offices of Will Hays and Joseph Breen. Her silver-blond mane and hoarse, predatory purr had furnished an insidious antidote to the bright-eyed, perky heroines who had dominated the industry before Pearl Harbor. This, according to the subtext, was what had become of the "gentler sex" while the men were away at the front.

The bedroom, done entirely in cream and black and as big as a warehouse, was scarcely large enough to contain the enormity of death.

Fresh flowers bloomed unaware in a vase on a low dresser forested with unposed family pictures in silver frames. A pair of fuzzy pink slippers on the floor beside a bed shaped like a sleigh, and a pale pink silk dressing gown draped over the foot-board, awaited their mistress. Here the only item pertaining to the movies was the honorary Oscar presented to her years before by the Academy as an apology for having passed over her finest performances in favor of ponderous costume dramas and glossy musical extravaganzas; in the world of pompous prestigious showboaters, no "melodramas" need apply. The award looked lonely on its corner of a mirror-topped vanity table. A framed certificate commemorating her efforts on behalf of the World Hunger Foundation occupied a much more prominent position on the wall just inside the door.

Was this a woman who could have arranged Van Oliver's murder, merely because she suspected him of edging her out of the *Bleak Street* cast? But a realist like Kyle Broadhead would have reminded him of the good deeds performed by the worst offenders, and the worst transgressions committed by the most celebrated humanitarians. Stereotypical casting existed only on the soundstage; people were invariably more complex and inexplicable than they were represented in screenplays.

The three were not alone with the deceased. As they entered, a man and woman seated next to the bed looked up at them with barren eyes. The man was gray-haired, dressed somewhat flashily in stacked lapels and a yellow silk handkerchief, and might have been considered large in any company that didn't include the hulking Vivien. The woman was a few years younger and wore plain slacks and a sweater and no makeup. Her brown hair was cut short.

"Dale Grant, Miss Lane's nephew," said Ms. Tanner. "His wife, Louise. This is Mr. Valentino."

"Valentino will do," said Valentino.

Grant rose and offered a listless hand. "Are you a policeman?"

He shook his head. That made twice in half an hour he'd

been mistaken for the law. "Just an admirer. With your permission I'd like to pay my respects."

"Don't tell me it's on the news already," said Grant. "I wouldn't have thought Aunt Ivy was such good copy. It's been so long since she was in the public eye."

Ms. Tanner said, "Valentino is here by invitation."

Grant's brow puckered. "That's odd. She was scrupulous about keeping commitments. Even despondent as she must have been, she'd have thought it rude. I know that sounds fatuous, but—" He spread his hands, at a loss to complete the sentence.

Valentino finished it for him. "—a person like that would be more likely to put off her plans in order to accommodate an expected visitor; even plans for her own death."

He was acutely aware that four pairs of eyes were staring at him; but his own were fixed on the small still figure in the bed.

19

VALENTINO FORCED HIMSELF to be objective, to see an elderly woman and not a figure of glamour created by experts in makeup, lighting, and filters.

True, age had scored and lengthened the face that had seduced half the second string of leading men; yet the features were girlish in repose. Her hair, tinted a lighter shade of yellow now to conceal the gray, was arranged in a demure braid over her left shoulder. She wore a plain flannel nightgown and her slim hands, the veins coarsened by time, were nearly as pale as the cream-colored spread upon which they rested.

"Did she leave a note?"

Georgia Tanner shook her head. She, too, was watching the inert face, as if waiting for the eyes to open and the expression to change: *Don't count me out yet.* "She wasn't much for writing, notes or letters. When a man came from AFI asking if she'd consider donating her papers, she said, "'What papers? I'm an actress, not a scientist.'"

"I'm still not buying this," Grant said. "I just saw her last week. She was as chipper as ever."

"These decisions are often made on the spur of the moment, Dale," said the attorney. "I don't think she ever forgave the industry for tossing her on the scrapheap when she turned forty. There's talk of remaking *Carlotta*, with Cameron Diaz, of all people. That was Ivy's signature role. It must have eaten at her, though she wouldn't show it. I was here last night, and she seemed fine then; but let's not forget she was an actress."

"Perhaps you're right. Well, maybe she'll have her moment back in the spotlight now. Too bad she can't enjoy it. She only pretended to be a recluse in order to attract attention." Grant's throat worked. "If you'll excuse me." He hurried out. His wife remained in her seat for an undecided moment, then got up and followed him.

"He loved his aunt very much," Georgia Tanner said. "He came here to have brunch with her. He took the news badly. I think he's only in denial because he's afraid he'd be furious with her for what she did. You never know what form grief will take."

"Is he a bitter man usually?"

"Only with himself. I understand there was a row when he dropped out of medical school and went into business. Things were never the same between them after that. Not that they ever spoke of it when I was around. Louise let it slip once. She doesn't say much, but when she does it's usually indiscreet."

"Was his aunt as vain as he said?"

"Not among friends and family, but she enjoyed putting on a show for strangers. She said people who came to see Ivy Lane expected an event, and she wasn't about to disappoint them. That would explain why she agreed to see you."

"I wonder what changed her mind."

From far down the canyon came the sound of a siren. It echoed off the cliffs, which distorted it into a bone-chilling howl. It seemed to go on a long time, then suddenly whooped around the corner and growled to a halt at the base of the steps.

At least ten minutes passed before the doorbell rang. Valentino and Georgia Tanner followed Vivien to the foyer, where the big man opened the door on a pair of uniformed officers and more than six feet of equal opportunity employment in the person of Sergeant Lucille Clifford of Homicide.

She was wearing her sunset-red hair above the shoulders now, but retained the stern towering air of an ambulatory Statue of Liberty. She stood straight as a pike in a powder-blue blazer cut long enough to conceal her service revolver, a black knee-length skirt, black-and-white pumps with modest heels, and her gold shield on a folder clipped to an outside pocket.

If the film archivist had hopes she'd mellowed since their last encounter, her first words dashed them to pieces.

"Glad I'm not with the coroner. I'd hate to be the one to carry a stiff down those stairs." She spotted Valentino. "You."

"Sergeant. Isn't this outside your beat?"

"We don't pound beats anymore, Boston Blackie. Don't carry Roscoes or pinch apples neither. In cases of sudden death— suicide, trip and fall, an alien in the belly—it's any Homicide detective in a storm. But since you brought it up, this one's a little fresh for you, isn't it? You usually don't come in until forty years after the body heat ran out."

"This time it's coincidence—maybe. I'm still working on whatever became of Van Oliver. He and Ivy Lane had a history."

"Of course they did. I've been waiting for the other shoe to drop ever since you borrowed the file."

A paw like a steam shovel landed on Valentino's shoulder.

"Kind of chummy with L.A.'s finest, ain't we? What're you, one of them pervs gets his jollies browsing the morgue?"

"Vivien!" snapped the Tanner woman.

"I don't trust this bird." But the hand was withdrawn.

"Pardon my glove, Sasquatch." Clifford slid in past him. To Tanner: "If I were you, I'd trust your big friend's instincts. Are you the one who called?"

"Yes." She made introductions. Dale and Louise Grant had joined them.

"Vivien; seriously?"

The bodyguard clenched his jaw. "My friends call me Bull."

"Okay, Mr. Broderick." The sergeant identified herself and the officers. One's surname was Howard, the other's Harold. Harold was black, Howard white; or was it the other way around? To Valentino they were as alike as opposite pieces on a chessboard.

Tanner filled them in on the way to the bedroom. There, Clifford glanced at the body with no show of interest, then made a silent signal. She and the officers split up to examine the room. The inlaid ebony dresser was full of extravagant evening gowns, the walk-in closet a riot of rainbow silk and satin negligees on padded hangers. Some still had price tags. Howard and Harold wrote in pads.

Returning to the bed, the sergeant slid a gold pencil from an inside pocket, inserted it in the empty prescription bottle lying on its side on the nightstand, and lifted it to eye level. She read aloud the physician's name printed on the label. Harold and Howard recorded it. She put it back in the original position.

"Mr. Grant," she said, "were you her only living relative?"

Georgia Tanner spoke. "Yes. There was a son by her first marriage, but he was killed in Iraq."

This met with a stony look. "Impressive. His lips didn't even move."

The attorney flushed. "Force of habit, sorry. I represent the family."

"This is an informal interview, Counselor. Nice house. Does it go with the inheritance?"

Grant answered this time. "I've no idea. I haven't seen a will. I don't even know there is one."

"Ms. Tanner?"

She nodded. "There is. At the behest of my client, I can't disclose the details until the reading."

"Uh-huh. I suppose you come in for a commission."

Vivien stepped in front of Clifford. He had two inches on her and at least sixty pounds. "That ain't no way to talk."

She didn't twitch a muscle. "What's a bodyguard's devotion worth in dollars and cents?"

It might have been Valentino's imagination, but it seemed to him the man had begun to swell and turn green. Officers Harold and Howard took a step in Vivien's direction; but Clifford remained immobile, her smoky blue eyes fixed on Vivien's face as if she were looking at a sample on a microscope slide.

Ms. Tanner crossed her arms. "For your information, Lieutenant—"

"Sergeant. I work for a living."

"Noted. Ivy's third husband went through what was left of her fortune thirty years ago. Aside from this house and property, her Social Security pension was all she had, and most of that went into taxes and upkeep. I charged her a minimal fee to manage her affairs. As an officer of the court, I understand it's your job to eliminate all the possibilities, but—"

"I'm glad you understand. Where's a good room where I can conduct interviews?"

To his surprise, Valentino was her first subject. They sat on a pair of floral-print chairs in a small sun room, rattan blinds shielding them from the strong light coming through the west-facing windows. She crossed her legs and rested her hands in her lap. "Give me all of it."

He took that literally; always a sound policy when dealing with her. He began with Ignacio Bozal's bargain, *Greed* in return for *Bleak Street*, Valentino's interest in the Van Oliver case, the near-miss outside Starbuck's, and the morsel of information he'd gotten from Roy Fitzhugh that had brought him to Ivy Lane's house. He withheld nothing, not even the detail he'd kept from Kyle Broadhead to avoid ridicule. Finally he recapped his conversation with the others in the bedroom. She listened without changing expression and took no notes.

"People step off curbs into traffic every day," she said. "Sometimes they don't get run over. I think your friend the professor's right. It's probably nothing."

"He argued the other side, too."

"He should run for governor. So you think the guy looked like Oliver. Even if he's still around, he wouldn't look like himself. This state's rotten with bad drivers. We've cornered the market on sunny-ots."

"What's a sunny-ot?"

"An idiot that follows the sun till it sets in California."

"But what are the odds Ivy Lane would wind up dead the very day I was to ask her about her fight with Oliver?"

"This isn't Vegas. There are no odds."

"But—"

She uncrossed her legs, leaned forward, and patted his hand. She couldn't have astonished him more if she'd asked him out on a date. "Listen and learn."

At her instruction, the two men in uniform conducted the others into the room one at a time. Valentino stood in a corner trying to be unobtrusive as each took his old seat and answered questions. He couldn't tell which were significant and which were just to establish a pattern, like the innocuous queries posed during a lie-detector test. Clifford's was a highly specialized art. The sessions were brief and took place only minutes apart.

She saved the bodyguard for last. When he sat, his platter-sized hands resting on his thighs, the chair disappeared. Throughout the interview he kept casting suspicious glances Valentino's way.

"Was Grant here last night?" Clifford asked.

"No. This is the first time him and Mrs. Grant have been in all week."

"Does he have a key?"

"Sure. He's her nephew. But nobody comes in or goes out without me knowing."

"Where do you sleep?"

"Other end of the hall from Ms. Lane."

"Did she know about your record?"

He turned his face, black with rage, toward Valentino, who met it with blank shock.

"I'm clean," he said, turning back. His hands closed on his thighs, the knuckles white. "I paid my debt."

"I know. I'm the one who booked you. I might forget a face, but not sitting on that body, and with the name Vivien. I was on road patrol then. You blew four-point-oh on the Breathalyzer. You'd had your license yanked what, three times?"

"Twice. I ain't had a drop in ten years."

"That'd be just about the time you came to work for Ivy Lane."

"Yeah. I told her all about it. She said it was nothing to her so long as I kept my nose clean, and that I done. I might not of done it for anybody else, but I done it for her."

"Okay."

He kneaded his thighs. Valentino doubted those wrinkles would come out. "Okay?"

"Do I need to spell it? You're off the hook, Bull. Send Grant back in, will you?"

The nephew came in, but he didn't sit. "Did you forget something?" he said.

"One question, Grant. How'd you do it?"

20

"DO WHAT?" GRANT'S big heatlamp-tanned face was flat.

"Don't say anything more, Dale." Georgia Tanner came in, practically sprinting. Clearly she'd been eavesdropping from outside the door. She glared down at Clifford. "You won't get far boosting your arrest record when you have no chance of obtaining a conviction. Weren't you listening when I said Ivy's estate wasn't worth committing murder to acquire?"

"You're the first one to bring up murder, Counselor. I'm tempted to think there's a reason it was on your mind; but that would look like I *was* only interested in making a bust. But since it's on the table, a house this size on two acres in one of the most exclusive neighborhoods in a town with the highest property values in the world? How much was the last offer?"

The attorney's eyes dilated behind her glasses. "I didn't say—"

"It's California, sister. Everyone wants to live here, even Republicans."

"Twelve million. She told the agent she'd burn the place

down before she'd let some Arab potentate house his harem in her garden."

"Was Grant present when the offer was made?"

The nephew's face darkened. He took a step toward her chair. A hand squeezed his shoulder, stopping him. Valentino knew what that grip felt like. Vivien had entered, followed closely by Louise Grant, as silent as ever.

"I know how you did it," Clifford said. "I just wanted to see if I could jolt you into blurting it out, but you've got a smart lawyer. Did you think I wouldn't know what to look for in an O.D. case? Did you think even if I missed it, the medical examiner would too? The skin around even the tiniest punctures discolors and swells as a body's temperature goes down."

Valentino said, "But you barely glanced at the body."

"I knew what to look for, and where to look. In most cases of this type, it's in the jugular." To Grant: "Last night, after Georgia Tanner left and you were sure your aunt and her watchdog were asleep, you let yourself in, using your key, and dissolved a lethal dose of Seconal into a solution. It's my guess you came here already loaded for bear. We'll search your place for any pills you may have left behind. You'd know how much to use from your med-school training, and anyone can get hold of a hypodermic."

Vivien chimed in. "I'm a light sleeper. Seems to me I'd of heard something."

"Not unless there was a struggle. Being family, Grant knew where she kept the pills. He smeared his prints, because to wipe them off would've ruled out suicide, and dumped the pills down the sink. A million dollars for ten minutes' work is good wages even by Hollywood standards."

Grant boiled over. "This is pure guesswork! Worse, it's slander! I'll—"

Tanner shushed him.

Clifford looked at her. "You should take your own advice, Counselor. We'll be asking you again whether you disclosed the terms of the will to Grant."

Flushing again, Tanner said, "I may have mentioned something; to Mrs. Grant. She confided to me that she was worried about her husband's business. I—I sometimes think I'm part of this family. Louise is the worrying type. I wanted to comfort her. I swore her to secrecy," she added, with a glance Louise Grant's way.

"You can trust a spouse to keep a secret, if one of them is dead." The sergeant returned her attention to Grant. "You forgot one thing: Ivy Lane's nightgown. Tanner said she liked to put on a show for strangers, and you said yourself your aunt enjoyed being the center of attention. She had a closet full of beautiful negligees. The woman you both described would never have taken her own life in plain flannel."

A bellow shattered the tension in the room; it was the cry of a mortally wounded grizzly. Vivien reached down from his great height, snatched Grant's stacked lapels in his enormous hands, and lifted him off the floor. Grant gulped for air.

"Put him down!"

Four heads swiveled toward Louise Grant. The nephew's wife had an open purse in one hand and a hypodermic syringe in the other. She held the needle in an underhand grip like a switchblade. The point glittered.

"Put him down or I'll stick this in your kidney." Her thin, drawn face was feral.

Harold and Howard, who'd been hovering inside the doorway, stepped toward her. They stopped at a gesture from the sergeant.

The bodyguard lowered her husband to the floor and let go. Grant clawed the yellow handkerchief out of his pocket and mopped his face.

Clifford's head moved less than a hundredth of an inch. In less time than that took, one of the officers had Louise Grant in a chokehold and the other wrested the weapon from her hand before she could react.

The sergeant repeated the movement. The arm was withdrawn from the woman's throat, but the officers remained at her side, muscles flexed.

"She wouldn't die."

Everyone else was silent, watching Louise Grant. Her face now was drained of energy, her voice entirely without emotion.

"She was going to outlive us all. Dale's business was failing. She could have sold the house, bailed him out, and had plenty left over, but she refused. I pleaded with her. She said he should have considered the consequences when he dropped out of medical school."

"Louise." Grant twisted his handkerchief between his fists.

"I knew you'd never do it. She made you dance to her tune, the same way she manipulated all her leading men. It was no act. I was a registered nurse when I married you. Remember how refreshed you felt this morning? I spiked your tea last night with Seconal. I was gone for over an hour with your key to this house and you slept right through it."

"Cuffs," Clifford told the officers. "Miranda. There's a lawyer present, remember."

The forensics team came—Harriet wasn't with it, but it was a big detail—and the sergeant's work was finished for the time being. Valentino offered her a lift back to West Hollywood. The unmarked car she'd come in was crowded with Harold, Howard, and their prisoner. Clifford frowned at the compact's tires, but climbed into the passenger's seat.

He drove. "How'd you guess it?"

"'Guess'? Just for that I should issue you a citation for those baldies we're rolling on. You think we dumb flatfeet can't crack a case without Inspector Pinchbottom and the Little Rascals? We flag more killers in a week than Ellery Queen did in his whole career. Plus we're real."

"I don't suppose I could ask you to crack mine."

"And spoil your fun? One thing." She looked straight ahead. "What I said before, about coincidences; don't bet the farm on that. If Van Oliver was killed under contract—even if Ivy Lane did arrange it—the statute of limitations doesn't apply. As long ago as that was, there may be someone still around who knows enough to be dangerous."

He guided the car a block in silence. "Thank you."

"Well, don't get all mushy about it. I didn't cross my fingers when I swore to serve and protect. That means everyone, even walk-ons billing themselves as detectives. We should've trade-marked the name a hundred years ago."

They were at the station. She said, "Don't get dead, okay?"

"Well, thanks, Sergeant. I didn't know you cared."

"Sure I do. I got corpses stacked six deep, a husband who thinks I threw him over for the M.E., and a kid who half the time calls me by my sister's name. If you do get dead, try to do it on the sheriff's time." She got out.

Like mad dogs, Englishmen, and the sun, Angelinos rarely miss an opportunity to enjoy a starry night. Valentino's quarters, in the concrete bunker of a fireproof projection booth, had no windows, so after dark he went to the terrace to howl at the moon; or at least to look at it.

As he did so, his silhouette showing against the light spilling out the open door, a movement across the street below caught his eye. A figure that had been standing under a streetlamp turned into a dark doorway. In the process, Valentino saw a face lifted to the spot where he stood gripping the wrought-iron railing. There was no doubting it this time: The man wearing a trench coat and snapbrim hat could have doubled for Van Oliver in his prime; a dead ringer in every sense of the phrase.

III

OUT OF THE PAST

21

THAT SATURDAY HAD been set aside for months: Harriet wanted to take in the annual Renaissance Fair in Agoura's Paramount Park. Valentino, who preferred as a rule to limit his theme-park experience to the Universal Studios tour, had agreed, but only because a tent showing had been arranged there for the newly restored *Black Shield of Falworth*, a prize he'd narrowly lost to Supernova International.

"Tony Curtis as a medieval knight?" she'd asked. "'Yonder lies the castle of my fadda'?"

"He never said that; it's just another myth, like Cagney saying, 'You dirty rat.' But, yes. Mostly I like Torin Thatcher as the master of knights. I think Alec Guinness took notes when he was prepping for Obi-Wan Kenobi."

"What costume will you wear?"

"Do we have to? I mean, isn't that for kids?"

"What are we, Ma and Pa Kettle?"

So he put on a leather jerkin and a hat with a feather in it, courtesy of the wardrobe department at Warner Brothers; the outfit had faded from its original Lincoln green and smelled of moth flakes, but the sewn-in label bore the name of Errol Flynn's stunt double. He felt a little less foolish when Harriet came to her door in tights and a laced corset. At least nobody would be looking at him.

They walked out on *The Black Shield of Falworth* before the end of the first reel. He was steaming. She laced her arm inside his.

"Sorry, Val. I blame social media. Parents need to teach their brats to keep their opinions to themselves during the campy parts, at least in public."

He patted her arm. "It's okay. I guess it is kind of a dumbed-down *Ivanhoe.*"

"You've got it on DVD, right? We'll watch it in The Oracle."

"If that isn't true love, I don't know what is."

She laid her head on his shoulder. A knock-kneed jester with a neck tattoo scowled at them and said, "Hie thee to a room!"

In the commissary they dined at a trestle table on a mutton joint (Valentino; actually a lamb shank) and roast boar (Harriet; actually a BLT), while jugglers and tumblers performed to the lively strains of a trumpet and lute. After the entertainers exited, he filled her in on his investigation, finishing with the mysterious stranger he'd spotted across from the theater.

"A trench coat and fedora?" she said. "You're kidding, right?"

"It didn't seem so funny last night."

"Did you notify the police?"

"I just did."

"What am I going to do, track him down, dissect him, and weigh his brain?"

"Thanks." He put down his knife and fork and pushed away his plate.

"You know what I mean."

"What could they do? This morning I checked out that doorway. It belongs to a restaurant closed for renovation. There weren't any Egyptian cigarette butts or darts dipped in African frog venom or bits of clay that can only be found in Argentina. I think someone's just trying to scare me off the case."

"You're an archivist, Val. You don't *have* cases. What do you think he'll do if he *can't* scare you off?"

He took a spoonful of mint jelly, testing his stomach's powers of recovery. "I'm no danger to anyone. Whoever's responsible for Oliver's vanishing act—if anyone is—he's either dead or too old to pose any kind of threat."

"Still, you should report it."

"They'd laugh me out of the station."

She bit into her sandwich, chewed, swallowed. "You're probably right. A guy dressed like a character out of Oliver's movie, in the last place in the country that needs a coat and hat of any kind? Who just happened to look up just as you stepped outside, so you could see his face clearly in the light? No one who meant you any harm would do that. You're right: Someone's just trying to spook you."

"It's working. That thing downtown was a close call."

"Yes, and I was about to drop a piano on you for keeping that from me when you got to that business across the street. I still might."

"I didn't want you to worry in case it turned out to be nothing."

She pushed away her plate, the BLT unfinished. "Val, if we're not in this together, what are we?"

"You're right."

"This isn't the first time we've had this conversation."

"I know. I just—"

"What if some jerk almost ran me down and I kept it from you? How could I know it was an accident? Could be it was someone who knew I was connected with the police. It's open season on every department, the way the press plays it up every time someone accuses a cop of stepping out of bounds."

He watched an ogre climbing off the bench belonging to the neighboring table. His green mask was still peeled up from his mouth so he could eat. "I never thought of it that way."

"I can't keep walking you through the steps of a relationship. You can't just jump-cut to another scene when it suits you."

He smiled. "I love it when you talk dirty."

"Don't even try changing the subject that way. You're not Kyle." She plucked a chickpea (the chalkboard menu referred to it as "grapeshot") off his plate and ate it. "You think Fitzhugh was right and Ivy Lane had something to do with what happened to Oliver?"

"You know what?" He brightened. "I'm going to go with that: The circumstances of her death are sure to be public knowledge by tonight. *Access Hollywood* thrives on that stuff. It's just the kind of publicity angle Henry Anklemire can run with."

"Accusing someone who isn't here to defend herself, on no evidence but an old man's suspicions? That's not like you."

He chewed morosely. "You're right, of course. Well, I'm through with it. I've taken the thing as far as I can. Whoever my ghost is, he can haunt someone else. Meanwhile we'll finish duping *Bleak Street* and hope Turkus will change his mind about releasing it."

"Let's drink a hearty quaff of mead in honor of that decision." She lifted her tankard.

He clanked his against it and sipped. "I never knew ye olde knights of olde drank anything that tasted so much like Diet Pepsi."

Waiting for her outside a portable restroom, Valentino saw something that stirred the mutton in his stomach. He crossed a long line waiting in front of a food truck and laid his hand on the epauleted shoulder of a figure in a trench coat with a hat pulled low over his forehead. The figure started and turned. It was a boy of seventeen or eighteen with a pearl in his nose that looked like a giant zit. Valentino turned his palms up in apology and walked back the way he'd come. America's youth had a lot to learn about what constituted Renaissance wear.

On Monday, he dropped by the lab. Jack Dupree, sporting a white smock in place of his heavy-duty chemical wear, came out of the restricted area, looking less greenish under his dark pigment than he had the day after the celebration in the Bradbury Building.

"Looks like Dr. Broadhead's Elixir cleared away the alcoholic clouds," Valentino said in greeting.

"That, and the ice-cold beer I had for breakfast."

"Any progress on *Bleak Street*?"

The smile evaporated. "You know, we moved it up on the schedule as a favor to you and Broadhead. Practical jokes don't fly in cases like that."

"What kind of practical joke?"

Dupree studied his expression. "Let's go to the movies."

Gone was the old screening room with linoleum floors, folding chairs, a roll-up screen, and a projector on a squeaky cart. Thanks in no small part to some high-profile discoveries made by Valentino, alumni donations had paid for a soundproof chamber with blackout walls and ceiling, graduated seats, interchangeable high- and negative-gain screens, noise-absorbing carpeting, a ten-channel stereo receiver, concert-class speakers, and acoustic diffusers that reflected sound evenly in all directions. This was no plush theater like Ignacio Bozal's or The Oracle, but a room intended strictly for the scientific study of film, as up-to-the-minute as a NASA control room. Equipment designed to project both digital and analog images made it possible to view either Julia Roberts or Greta Garbo at the top of their form, in sharper focus than the originals.

Some things never changed, however. At Kyle Broadhead's insistence, the university kept a certified projectionist on permanent retainer, not to please the union so much as to ensure the proper handling of his department's most valuable properties. This one kept sentry in a booth above the top row in back.

Dupree sat down beside Valentino in the center sweet spot. "Roll 'em, Sid!" To the archivist: "The can said '*Bleak Street*, Reel One.'"

Minutes later they watched a lively figure whistling as he steered a boat, spinning the spoked helm and tugging a steam whistle. The character was instantly recognizable in the most remote corners of the world, and had been seen by more people than George Washington, Napoleon, Shirley Temple, Mao Tse-Tung, and Oprah Winfrey combined.

"*Steamboat Willie*," Valentino whispered. "What—?"

Dupree said, "I prefer to call him Mickey. I've been on a first-name basis with him since I was ten. That's when my parents took me to Disneyland the first time. Okay, Sid!"

The film stopped fluttering through the gate and the screen went white. The lab technician turned to Valentino. "Is there anything you want to tell me?"

22

"**KYLE, I NEED** your help."

"Does it have anything to do with Van Oliver?"

"It has *everything* to do with Van Oliver."

"Can't do it, sorry."

"Kyle—"

"Can't, son. My gat's in the shop. The guy offered me a loaner but I said I'd be better off without it for a while. I made a New Year's resolution to give up gambling and stop shooting people."

"You don't gamble."

"Then I'm halfway there. Call your buddy Anklemire. He's a smaller target."

"All I need is some advice."

"Give it up. How's that?"

"Kyle, I'm coming over. You can turn me down to my face."

"Nope. I'm on a fishing boat in Catalina."

"No, you're not. I called you at home. You don't own a cell."

"Nuts. I won't answer the door."

Something clicked. Valentino thought he'd hung up. Then Fanta's voice came on. "Come on over, Val. I'll put on coffee."

Broadhead said, "Get off the extension!"

Valentino said, "I didn't know you were home."

"The defense wants to settle the copyright infringement case I was working on. I got the day off."

"Blast you, woman! I'm going to the club."

"Shut up, old man," she said. "They kicked you out for non-payment of dues before I was born."

Valentino said he was on his way.

Kyle Broadhead seldom went to his office on Monday. He'd lived in a Wilson-era clapboard bungalow in a neighborhood that had gone downhill after the motion-picture colony moved to Beverly Hills and Malibu, then came back when the population swelled between world wars, then slid again during the era of sex, drugs, and rock-and-roll, but had commenced to climb up again with gentrification. In Valentino's experience the professor had always kept it up, painting it a cheery yellow every few years, replacing the roof and windows, and overpaying a succession of youths to cut the grass; but since his marriage to Fanta, lilac bushes and beds of iris and poppies the bright orange of crepe paper had transformed it into a modest showplace. Valentino parked in a driveway the couple shared with the house next door, wiped his feet on a crisp new welcome mat, and pushed the bell.

Fanta, tall and tan in a sleeveless white top knotted at her midriff, yellow shorts, and flip-flops, gave him a hug and dragged him over the threshold by the hand. "Welcome, stranger. This is the first time you've honored us since the wedding. I was afraid you'd dropped us when I made an honest man out of Kyle."

"I'm—"

"For the love of Mike, don't apologize!" came a voice from the little den off the living room. "The whole reason I gave H.R. only a P.O. box for my checks was to keep the university away from my door. If it gets out we invited anyone from work, everyone but the janitor will follow the trail and the next thing you know we'll be throwing Christmas parties."

"This is what I live with, Val."

"I warned you, as I recall." He followed her into the den.

Broadhead was sitting in the dilapidated overstuffed chair that had held court in the living room from the time he'd moved in until Fanta arrived. He wore a dingy gray cardigan blown out at the elbows, baggy slacks, and heelless slippers on his feet. In front of him, a portable TV set with rabbit ears sat on a combination TV, radio, and phonograph in a console the size and shape of a coffin. Both sets were on with the sound turned down. A baseball game made up of all Japanese players took place on the larger screen, with what looked like a curling competition on the portable, both in silence.

"I didn't know you were into sports," Valentino said.

"Not since the introduction of the designated hitter and the reviewed play. I only turn on a game because people keep interrupting my reading." He marked his place in the book in his lap with a finger.

"He's talking about me," Fanta said. "He's formed the conclusion that if he pretends to be watching, I won't disturb him."

"You agreed to that?"

"Humor him in the things that don't count, so I can nag him into the things that do; like not blowing off friends when they come to him for help."

"That's not settled," Broadhead said.

She leaned down and kissed him on the top of his shaggy head. "Coffee's almost ready." She went out and drew the door shut.

Valentino took in the den. It was cluttered with items that had occupied the living room during Kyle's widowerhood, including a large pewter urn on the mantel of a small gas fireplace. "Is that—?"

"The late Mrs. Broadhead, yes. I wanted to move it out before the honeymoon; I even looked into reserving a space next to her favorite stars in Forest Lawn; by-the-by, Marilyn Monroe's booked for blocks. Fanta wouldn't have it. Some nonsense about not erasing my past just because I've discovered the future."

"That sounds like the kind of advice you give your students."

"Turn those things off, will you? They didn't come with remotes."

Valentino switched off the TVs. The pictures imploded and the screens went black. He sat on the arm of a love seat that faced Broadhead's chair at an angle; the cushions were piled with framed pictures, a loose collection of briar pipes, and ashtrays banished from around the house since it had turned into a place of cohabitation. Somehow it all seemed of a piece with the professor's lifestyle: Stark and organized at work, chaotic at rest. He listened to the latest development with his lids lowered and his hands folded across his middle, Buddha fashion.

"*Steamboat Willie* wouldn't fill five reels," he said.

"I only saw part of one, but Jack Dupree says the others were a hodgepodge of comedy shorts, newsreels, and out-of-date travelogues. Batista's Cuba sounds like a fun place to spend a weekend, but only if you're a *Yanqui*."

"You're sure the film cans were never out of your sight from the time Bozal gave them to you until you put them in storage?"

"I am; and department security has never been compromised in the past."

"The conclusion being that Bozal switched the reels sometime between the private screening and when he gave you the cans."

"To state the obvious, yes."

"There's nothing so obscure as the obvious, boys."

Both men looked up at Fanta, who had managed to open the

door while carrying a loaded tray without drawing attention. Valentino sprang up to clear rubble off a square ottoman, took the tray, and placed it on the leather seat. The room would not sit three, but she waved off the visitor's offer to clear the love seat and lifted the steel carafe to pour.

"The trouble with you academic types is you see everything as up and down, left and right," she said, handing out the steaming mugs. "If you ever spent any time in a courtroom you wouldn't be so sure. Motive's everything. Bozal wanted to trade *Bleak Street* for *Greed*, correct?"

"That was the arrangement." Valentino sat back down with his coffee.

"Then why renege? From what you've told us about him, he's not the kind to take foolish chances. He had to have known you'd screen the film again before you delivered on your end."

"Nothing obscure about that." Broadhead's tone was dry.

"Any judge in the district would throw your case against him out of court during the preliminary." She looked at Valentino. "Did you actually *see* Bozal put the reels in the cans before he gave them to you?"

"No. As a matter of fact—" He fell silent.

"What?" This in unison from Fanta and Kyle.

"Just a thought." He stood and set his coffee on the tray untasted. "Thanks, both of you."

Fanta said, "You're going out there, aren't you? East L.A."

"I'll call first."

She smiled. "When I invite myself to someone's house, I always bring a gift."

When that sank in, Valentino smiled too.

As arranged over the phone, Jack Dupree met him at the door of the secure storage facility next to the lab with an oversize gym bag in his arms. The technician's face asked a question. Valentino shrugged an answer, thanked him, and slung the bag over his shoulder by its strap. It was heavy.

A female voice answered the phone at Ignacio Bozal's house: low-pitched, with a slight Hispanic accent. He recognized it.

"My grandfather's napping, Mr. Valentino. May I take a message?"

"I'd like to visit, if he has time this afternoon. I have something for him. He'll know what it is."

He wished he could see Esperanza Bozal's face. Her tone was hard to interpret over the wire. "I'm sure he'll be happy to see you."

Outside, he started down the street to the north lot, where he'd parked. An automobile slowed and turned into the curb as if to let someone out. The driver's side door swung open, blocking his path. The man who stepped out stood well over six feet tall. His charcoal-gray suit was tailored; had to be, to contain his chest and shoulders. Valentino looked from him to the vehicle. It was a black, slab-sided town car with shuttered headlights.

23

THE DRIVER, AT least, bore no resemblance to the man who had nearly run him down and who had skulked in the shadows outside The Oracle; but his size and fierceness of expression weren't encouraging.

When he spoke, however, his voice was light, despite the echo chamber that was his chest. "Get in the car, please."

Please? Not a word in the vocabulary of the usual run of hood that kidnapped citizens on the street in broad daylight. But as Bozal had said, the mob had developed subtle methods since Prohibition. Their victims' bodies seldom showed up in ditches anymore, for instance, but in the foundations of skyscrapers and football stadiums.

"Another time, maybe. I'm in a hurry." He turned to go around the man, only to be stopped by a hand on his arm; not as big a hand as Vivien "Bull" Broderick's, nor the grip as punishing, but not one to be shaken off easily.

What would Humphrey Bogart or Robert Mitchum say in this situation; or Woody Allen, for that matter? He had nothing to lose.

"I know someone who's bigger than you are."

The man nodded. His face was grave. "I believe you. I was two months' premature. Thirty-one ounces at birth. There's no telling how far I'd have developed if I'd gone full term." He dropped the hand. "Five minutes. I promise."

Valentino was pondering just how much damage could be inflicted on a person in five minutes when the window belonging to the rear passenger's seat hummed down and the man seated there leaned his head out the window. "I'll drop you off anywhere you want, and send the car back for you when you're ready. Please." A latch clicked and the door opened.

He'd feared this was Van Oliver's ghost—or at least his double—but recognized the face from another time. It belonged to the man who'd once sprung him from police custody on an obstruction case over a property both men were in competition to acquire. Mark David Turkus, the man who'd built a teenage hobby he'd started in his parents' home into the biggest entertainment vendor in the world, had aged a bit—his trademark do-it-yourself haircut showed traces of gray, and creases had appeared around his plain black-rimmed glasses—but his face retained the *naïf* quality that had lulled so many of his competitors into underestimating his gift for ruthlessness. "The Turk," as they came to call him, *was* Supernova International, as surely as Johnny Weissmuller was Tarzan, Sean Connery James Bond, and Pee-wee Herman—well, Pee-wee Herman.

Turkus slid to the other side of the seat. The driver grasped the handle and swung the door wide.

Valentino climbed in and rested his hands on the bag in his lap. As soon as his body made contact with the buttery leather seat, he knew this wasn't the car that had nearly crushed him downtown. It was like comparing a dinghy to an ocean liner. There was room to stretch his legs without coming into contact with the front seat, and a complete portable bar straddled the upholstered hump above the transmission. Characteristic of his host's juvenile tastes, among the fifths of premium vodka, bourbon, and single-malt Scotch stood a two-liter bottle of Diet Dr Pepper.

The door snicked shut and the driver returned to his seat behind the wheel. Turkus tipped open the top of a built-in cooler and plunged a silver scoop into the ice. "Libation?" When Valentino declined, he filled a crystal tumbler with cubes and poured soda-pop inside slowly to control the fizzing. "My doctor says that if I insist on soft drinks, I should go with the full-leaded; sugar's more healthy than artificial sweetener. I'm used to it, though, and I make enough decisions without adding another. What's your position?"

"I don't have one."

Valentino realized then the car was moving; the motor was nearly silent, the suspension of the sort not to be found in any factory. Los Angeles slid past the tinted windows as smoothly as back-projection.

"He's head of surgery at the Mayo Clinic; but don't let that intimidate you." Turkus sipped at the effervescent beverage and belched discreetly into his fist. "A physician who carries five million in malpractice insurance is no one to fear, unless you're his patient. Where to?"

"Just circle around and drop me off at my car. That shouldn't take any longer than five minutes, even in this town." Valentino's knuckles whitened on the bag in his lap. A man with Turkus' resources and business savvy posed as much of a threat as a thug with a tommy gun.

"What've you got there? You're holding it like it's the key to Fort Knox. There's no gold there, by the way; the chairman of the joint chiefs of staff conducted me on a personal tour last year. The actual bullion is stored someplace ten stories underground; can't tell you where. The fort itself is just diversion:

spray-painted wooden blocks surrounded by marines in dress blues. Don't breathe a word of that to anyone," he whispered, leaning close. "It's a state secret."

"It's *Greed*."

"I'm sorry?"

Valentino patted the bag. "The von Stroheim film. I promised it to a friend. It's in general release now. *Bleak Street* is in secure storage, if that's what you're getting at." There was no sin in lying to the competition.

Mark David Turkus laughed; a juvenile laugh, not at all the sinister chuckle of the megalomaniac that Valentino had come to associate him with. It ended in a burp. "Excuse me. I don't want the film; for myself, I prefer musical extravaganzas, lots of glitz in bright high-key lighting. But I understand the appeal of the dark stuff. It's why Adolf Hitler's autograph is worth twenty times Winston Churchill's. My attorneys assure me *Bleak Street* is as safe from public viewing as if it were socked away with all that gold in—" He burped again. "Whoops. I almost spilled the beans. Anyway, ironclad doesn't signify. I make sure everything's in steel surrounded by concrete; am I right, Sean?"

The driver answered without looking away from the windshield. "Yes, sir."

Turkus' smile was boyish. It was one of his most lethal weapons. "Sean's one of my attorneys."

"He's not a bodyguard?"

"That'd be bad for my image. Only gangsters need bodyguards. I selected him on his academic record. He got into Harvard on a football scholarship. When he blew out his knee, he started reading Blackstone. Turned out he had a knack for the law. I asked him to drive only because I just found out today I forgot to renew my license." Turkus' face went serious then. "That film must never be exhibited."

For no reason that Valentino could identify, he sensed he

was being asked for help. He pressed the point before he could talk himself out of it.

"If you've tied it up so tight, why talk to me?"

"You don't let things go, that's why. You'll appeal the court ruling, and when it holds up you'll take it to the next court and the next, and even though you're bound to end in failure, the press will lap it up every step of the way. In this country, and especially in this town, when someone who's even marginally connected with the entertainment industry pushes an issue, the media take note. As a result, the thing someone has spent hundreds of thousands of dollars to keep quiet—and manages to do so legally—has a way of finding its way to the public, whether or not there's any evidence to support it. The result's the same. Someone's reputation is destroyed, along with thousands of lives that depend on it."

"Whose reputation are we talking about?"

Turkus pressed a toggle switch in his armrest. A Plexiglas shield slid up between the front and back seats. No doubt it was soundproof, but he lowered his voice anyway.

"Lawyer-client privilege is just a concept," he said. "You know it exists only when it's been violated. If you repeat this conversation to anyone and it gets back to me, as I assure you it will, you won't be able to get a job delivering pizza anywhere in this country. The same goes for your entire staff. Your girl-friend, Miss Johansen? Unemployed and unemployable; thanks to the anonymous donor who made it possible to replace all the onboard computers in the LAPD fleet with next year's model.

"Not enough? Okay. Everything you brought to the university will become the property of Supernova. Your entire department—the archives, the film library, the laboratory, and the screening facility—will cease to exist."

Valentino experienced the same chill he'd felt when he saw the phantom outside The Oracle. He swallowed—silently, he hoped. "I take it not telling me what you're about to tell me is not an option."

"No, because without an explanation you'd never give up. Even if you failed to find out what happened to Van Oliver, your meddling would revive enough interest to reopen the investigation, if not by the police then by the press. Regardless of whether anything definite comes of it, the muck they'll rake up will cling to everyone involved with what happened sixty years ago, however remotely. The stock in Supernova will plummet. Who'd place any faith in a business everyone is convinced is founded on murder? The board of directors would have no choice but to force me to resign."

The car stopped for the light at Hollywood and Vine. A mob of pedestrians in straw hats and loud sportshirts crossed the street in front of them, holding cell-phone cameras at arm's length trained on the signs identifying the historic corner. Valentino found himself lowering his voice as well.

"What does Supernova have to do with the Oliver case?"

Turkus subsided in his seat, hands dangling limp between his thighs. "My uncle, Constantine Venezelos Turkus; Connie, to his friends. His enemies called him something else. He was the original Turk. You know that saying, 'He knows where all the bodies are buried'? According to family lore it was Uncle Connie who buried them."

24

THE CAR GLIDED through neighborhoods Valentino knew intimately, but he could not have identified any of them. As Mark David Turkus spoke they seemed as foreign as craters on the moon.

The tycoon might have been retelling the plot of a movie he'd seen; but then that was the nature of this entire episode in the film archivist's life. No other quest had so closely resembled the grail he sought.

"Uncle Connie" had perfected his trade while serving with the U.S. Navy Shore Patrol during the First World War, rounding up AWOL sailors in New York City gin mills that had been declared off-limits by the local base commander and smashing the establishments to pieces. Eventually his superiors had decided that he was taking his job too seriously; he was court-martialed and given a dishonorable discharge.

With that stigma on his record, most legitimate employment was denied him. Just what kind of work he'd found to support himself was something the family preferred not to dwell upon. When he suddenly took the train to California, it seemed logical to assume it was either to avoid arrest or retribution on the part of his associates.

Official disgrace presented no obstacle to the employment he found on the coast. There, during the Great Depression, he founded a freelance security firm that hired itself out to all the major studios.

"The operatives were known as the Blackbirds," the billionaire said. "Maybe you heard of them."

"Strikebreakers, weren't they?"

"Not right away. They were hired originally to protect the stars from blackmail. In those days gangsters threatened to throw acid in their faces if they didn't pony up. A lot of those goons suddenly took to greener pastures, so it stands to reason the Blackbirds were longer on offense than defense.

"When that crisis ended, the firm branched out. The contract players were forming labor unions. Fair wages and acceptable terms cut into the studios' bottom line, so the Turk's men broke up meetings, shanghaied union organizers across the state line, and waded into picket lines with blackjacks and brass knuckles. They wore identical black suits to avoid roughing each other up by mistake; hence the nickname."

"They failed in the end," Valentino said. "The Screen Actors Guild is one of the most powerful in the country."

"Uncle Connie was no quitter. Kicking him out of the navy didn't stop him from doing the same work on the other side of the law. Having to flee the heat back East didn't scare him straight. When the mob backed off and the union survived, the Blackbirds went deeper underground, taking jobs the industry didn't dare do in-house."

"Such as?"

"Don't be naïve. What's it take to go from assault and battery to murder? Just a slight turn of the screw."

Twenty grim years passed, during which the elder Turkus

passed in and out of police headquarters as through a revolving door. The last time during his career was in connection with the questionable "suicide" of George Reeves, TV's Superman, in 1959.

"There were others that didn't make the front page, of course," said Mark Turkus. "Too many, I think, for him to be involved in most of them. The police even called him out of retirement to ask him about Bob Crane's murder in nineteen seventy-eight."

The *Hogan's Heroes* star. Valentino remembered the sordid details of a crime that was never solved.

Turkus went on. "The Black Dahlia case doesn't sound like him; but whenever powerful forces were involved, there was Connie's M.O., as big and fat as he himself got to be. As who wouldn't, on his commissions?

"I doubt he shared them all the time either," he added. "A man who worked himself up to the top doesn't mind getting his hands dirty."

There was more. In 1950, the Turk was arrested on suspicion of smuggling illegal aliens into the U.S. The theory was he delivered them to the studios to perform as extras, pocketing their wages in return for bringing them across the border. He spent three days in custody, then was released for lack of evidence.

"That was tame for him," said his nephew. "But he seems never to have passed up the chance to turn a fast buck."

"Wow."

"My legacy, I'm afraid. It's one of the reasons I always conduct business on the up-and-up. Even my fiercest competitors agree that at my most aggressive I've never violated any law. That would include you, I suppose."

Valentino had to give him that much, however much rope the system of free enterprise offered to pitiless entrepreneurs with unlimited funds.

"Was he ever brought to justice?"

The billionaire's smile was grim. "Only the Old Testament kind. He was diagnosed with terminal cancer in nineteen eighty-six and blew his brains out with his old service pistol. By then he'd been retired for twenty years."

"How well did you know him?"

"I only saw him once, at a family funeral. By then he was as big as a house. Here." He slid a flat wallet from an inside pocket, took out a creased Polaroid photograph, and handed it over.

It had been taken from a distance, on a plot of ground dotted with headstones in tidy rows. He was easy to spot in the soberly dressed crowd. The pinstripe suit did nothing to disguise a parade-float of a man whose jowls and multiple chins stood out from the shadow of his felt hat.

"I found it in my mother's collection of family snapshots," Turkus said. "I doubt she realized he was in the frame or she'd never have kept it. I carry it around as a reminder not to get too sweet on myself.

"He was my father's brother. They hadn't spoken in years, and they didn't on that occasion. No one was more surprised than I was when Uncle Connie left me twenty thousand dollars in his will."

"Why you?"

"Good question. I can't think he was driven by generosity. Maybe he did it to thumb his nose at the rest of his family. That was the seed money I used to start Supernova."

He raised his hands from his knees and spread them. "Now you know why I can't let you market *Bleak Street*."

"Does Teddie Goodman know?"

"She's my employee, not my confidante. I wouldn't have told *you* if I thought there was any other way of stopping you."

"What do you know about your uncle and Van Oliver?"

"Only that he was questioned along with a lot of others. I can thank the length of the list of suspects for keeping him off center stage. That won't be the case if the story gets raked up again. My name alone will put him square in the spotlight and the company with it." He lowered his hands, linked the fingers, and stared down at them. "It's not just me that would suffer. A public-relations blow like that would put thousands of people out of work and possibly trigger a national recession."

"But what was his motive?"

"Who knows? Maybe a mob contract, for whatever purposes. Like I said: anything for a buck."

"I wish you'd told me all this at the start."

"Would it have made any difference?"

"We'll never know now."

The car ghosted along for blocks, its occupants silent. Then Valentino said, "What if Constantine Turkus is cleared of any implication in the Oliver case? Would you lift the restraining order and allow UCLA to distribute the film?"

Mark David Turkus turned his attention from his hands clasped as in prayer to his fellow passenger. "No one can prove a man *didn't* do something. That's a basic law of nature."

"Of U.S. law too; that's why the prosecution has to prove guilt. In order to clear your uncle, I'll have to identify the real killer."

"After all this time, when all the experts have failed? And they called *me* a cock-eyed dreamer."

"You haven't answered my question."

"But what if it turns out Connie is the killer?"

"He's dead. It isn't as if sitting on the evidence would let a guilty man go free. No one would have to know."

They'd circled the campus and were approaching the spot where Valentino had been picked up. Turkus tapped on the Plexiglas and signaled the driver to pull over to the curb. He twisted in his seat to face the archivist. The corporate mask was back in place, rendering his face unreadable.

"Just so we're clear," he said. "If you manage to name the party behind Van Oliver's disappearance and it isn't Constantine Venezelos Turkus, you'll go public with it, closing the investigation for good. If it is my uncle, you'll suppress the information."

"That's what I'm offering."

"It's a gamble. Your silence alone would guarantee that the speculation will continue. It's bound to come around to him."

"I didn't say it wasn't risky. But apart from adopting Blackbird tactics, you won't stop me from seeing this through to the end. If it comes out in your favor, you'll never have to worry about Oliver again. And there's something else to be gained."

The eyes behind the glasses shone flatly, like plastic discs. So far as the man could be read at all, Valentino suspected he knew what was coming.

He didn't keep him in suspense. "You'll have peace of mind. If no capital crimes can definitely be laid to your family's door, you'll never have to wonder if your career was built on murder."

"Okay."

"Okay?"

"If you find out what happened to Van Oliver and who was responsible, Supernova will withdraw its suit and you'll be free to do what you want with *Bleak Street*; sell it, distribute it, burn it. The film is yours." He held out his hand.

Valentino grasped it. *Now if only I had it*, he thought.

25

VALENTINO GATHERED UP the gym bag containing all twenty-four hours of Erich von Stroheim's *Greed*. He held up the photograph. "May I keep this?"

"Please do. If everything works out as I'd like, I won't have to ask for it back."

"I'll be in touch." He opened the door and stepped out.

Mark David Turkus leaned over and took hold of the handle. "Mind you, I don't expect anything."

The archivist watched the sleek car sliding down the street. The motor made little more noise than when he'd been riding inside. By comparison, his compact sounded like a cement mixer starting up.

It was another day of brilliant sun, bringing out the green grass and red, yellow, and blue wildflowers in the Hollywood hills like bright scraps of construction paper. The vivid hues in the murals and graffiti in East L.A. were bolder yet, looking as if they'd been slapped on that morning with a brush dipped in a rainbow. He coasted to a stop before the gate in the parti-colored wall that enclosed the Bozal estate, and tooted his horn. The asthmatic bleating sound was a poor substitute for the virile blast of the old man's Bugatti.

The gate opened far enough for the young Chicano in the uniform to poke his head out.

"Hello, Ernesto. Your grandfather's expecting me."

A dazzling white grin split the medium-dark face. He spread the gate the rest of the way.

Everything was as before: children playing in shorts and nothing else, stout women minding them from their porch seats, young Antonio Banderas clones bent under open automobile hoods with heads cocked to keep the smoke from their cigarettes out of their eyes. It was as if four square blocks had drifted free of Guadalajara and come to rest a hundred miles north of the border, carrying with it several generations of Bozals.

Here again was the limestone turnaround at the end of the block, a half-century of classic cars drawn up bumper-to-bumper like circled wagons in a western, and beyond it the large plain house, like anyone might see in one of the better neighborhoods in Mexico: well-tended, unpretentious, and hinting at the cozy life under its roof. He found a spot behind a glistening cherry-red 1936 Cord, the emblem between its hidden headlamps and the historic plate establishing its make and vintage for the visitor.

The door was opened by the master of the house himself, his slight form dressed as casually as before in a rumpled sweater, flannel shirt buttoned to the neck, corduroys shiny at the knees, and scuffed slippers. His head of fine white hair was bare. At sight of the bag his guest was carrying, he exposed his perfect dentures all the way to the eyeteeth.

"I'd hoped," he said. "That's the dingus, right?"

Valentino laughed. The old man seemed to have been brushing up on his hard-boiled slang. "I wouldn't advise you to try watching it in one sitting. It's ten hours long."

"At my age I'm lucky to make it ten minutes without getting up to pee." Before Valentino could react, Bozal grasped the strap and pulled it from his grip.

His ninety-year-old constitution was remarkable. Leading his visitor toward the bar, he carried the bag as if it were a bundle of beach towels.

"Can I corrupt you, fella? Sun's not down past the yardarm." He stepped behind the bar, set down his burden, and picked up a cocktail shaker.

Valentino was about to decline; then he realized he hadn't had a drop of alcohol since the Bradbury party—was it only days ago?—and that he could use a drink. He was as far from an alcoholic as could be without becoming a total abstainer, but he understood the craving then.

"White wine, if you have it."

"Do I have it. Was W. C. Fields a lush?" He traded the shaker for a bottle with a Mondavi label and inserted a corkscrew. "You know he had more than fifty grand worth of booze socked away in his attic? This was during the Depression, when three bucks would get you a bottle of good bourbon."

"I never heard that about Fields."

"Take it or leave it, considering the source. I got it from Groucho Marx. Fields showed him the stash, he said."

"You knew Groucho?"

"Nobody did, really, except his brothers. I ran into him in the Brown Derby; we were with friends who knew each other. He was hosting *You Bet Your Life* at the time." He pulled the cork, filled a stemware glass, and slid it across the bar. Then he retrieved the cocktail shaker and mixed a vodka martini for himself.

Valentino took a healthy sip of wine. It was good Gewürztra-
miner, slightly sweet and pungent. He swallowed and waited for
his inhibitions to leave. "I screened *Bleak Street* again back at
the university. I couldn't resist." He studied Bozal's face closely
over the top of his glass.

The old man seemed to be engrossed in balancing a twist of
lemon on the edge of his own glass. "Knew you would. It's just
like chili."

"Like chili?"

"When you got the taste for it, it's all you want to eat till it's
gone. You won't need it again for a long time, you're sick of it,
but when you want it, nothing else'll do. It's that way with sex,
too; till you find the right woman. Then you can't ever get your
fill."

Was it a bluff? Did he think Valentino was bluffing? The
man was the Sphinx. Was everyone involved in this thing a
champion poker player except him?

It would take at least another drink to press him outright,
but Valentino didn't want to call attention to his unease. He
wandered around the room, carrying his wine; stopped before
the portrait above the mantel.

Estrella, Bozal's wife, dead these fifty years. Her beauty
reached across the decades as if she were standing in front
of him. He sipped again, barely conscious he was doing so. It
wasn't for courage.

"Forget it, kid."

He coughed, dribbling wine over his chin. Bozal's voice was
almost at his ear. He hadn't heard him coming up behind him.
Apologizing for his clumsiness, he brushed at the droplets on his
shirt.

"It's jake. Find myself doing it myself when I'm looking at
her. Forget it, I said. She was gone before you were born. She
won't come walking in on you from the rain like Laura. You're

a good-looking lad, but you're no Dana Andrews. Neither was he, when the camera wasn't cranking. He was a bad drunk off-screen, worse than Fields; when he took it on the set, he was through."

"You knew him too?"

"Hmm?" Bozal was looking at the painting, his martini untasted.

"You knew Dana Andrews?"

He turned away from the mantel with a jerk. "He came out of retirement for a bit in *The St. Valentine's Day Massacre*: Nineteen-sixty-seven, it was, but Roger Corman wanted it to look like 'twenty-nine. I rented him some clunkers from my fleet for the city exteriors. Andrews was on the set when I took charge of delivery. He was recovering then. Spilled it all to me, his battle with the bottle; me, a complete stranger. One of the twelve steps, I guess. Anyway it seemed to take. As far as I know he never touched another drop."

At any other time Valentino might have pressed the old man for more details, but he was scarcely listening. Something had begun to grow in his mind; something that had little if anything to do with whatever had happened to *Bleak Street*. It was absurd, fantastical, the stuff of a *noir* movie; but just what about this episode had not been? In any case it was too tentative to broach the subject just yet.

"Thank you for the wine. I'm sorry I can't finish it. I have a lot of work to do."

His host seemed surprised. "Shame to come all this way just to turn around and go back. I could've sent Eduardo to pick up *Greed*."

"It isn't that pressing," he lied. "But I need to show myself at the office now and then or they might think I'd defected to USC."

Bozal took the glass before the other could return it to the bar. "No need to explain, son. I'm grateful as all get-out. Them dagoes from the Vatican are sure to come across with what I need when I give 'em a private screening. You can't ever go wrong dishing up one of the Seven Deadlies to the clergy."

"Is Esperanza home? I'd like to see her before I go."

"Sure. She's on spring break. Your girl know about this?" He looked sly.

"It's not like that. I want to tell her what a good job she did in the projection booth." He assumed a pained look that wasn't all manufacture. "Sir, I thought you were a little hard on her at the time."

Bozal showed no trace of resentment. "She's known me all her life. If she's looking for the doting grandpa this late in the game she's got me miscast. Her room's at the top of the main staircase, on the right. Can't miss it: smells like a Tijuana cathouse clear down to the ground floor." The old man shook his hand, picked up the gym bag, and started in the direction of the door to the basement theater.

He felt oddly light-headed as he climbed the stairs from the tiled entrance, passing framed watercolors of the sun rising over the Gulf of Mexico and adobe walls in the moonlight. Confrontations were never his long suit, and beautiful women always brought out the awkward teenager he'd never quite outgrown, even when the women were not much more than half his age. Standing in front of the dark paneled oak door, he felt mad panic, like little Margaret O'Brien preparing to throw flour in the face of the neighborhood curmudgeon in *Meet Me in St. Louis*.

Get over it, Val. She's a college freshman, not the Spider Woman. He raised his fist and knocked.

The door opened almost instantly, as if the person on the other side were waiting just for him. The face he saw there emptied his head the rest of the way. He'd seen it twice before, but had never stood this close to young Van Oliver.

26

VALENTINO HAD COME face-to-face with a ghost; but he needed no mirror to know what his own face looked like. The man at the door stared, his eyes as big as pancakes.

"Who is it, Emiliano? Oh." Coming up behind him, Esperanza stopped, paling under her natural coloring.

In that moment Valentino was sure who it was who had substituted random footage for *Bleak Street,* and that Bozal knew nothing about it.

She touched the stranger's arm. *"Está bien, hermano."*

He stepped away from the door. Valentino entered and pushed it shut behind him.

Emiliano looked less mysterious than he had across the street from The Oracle. Gone were the hat and trench coat. He wore a black T-shirt with the AC/DC logo on the front, faded jeans artfully ripped at the knees, and flip-flops. Still, his facial resemblance to the young Van Oliver was uncanny.

Esperanza had changed from her red sheath to a tank top over pleated slacks, and from heels to pink high-top sneakers.

Her abundance of blue-black hair, high coloring, and bare brown shoulders were just as striking without the slinky outfit.

The room reflected her personality, with bright pink-and-black striped wallpaper, a rumpled bed with a canopy supported by minimalist black iron uprights, and posters of glamorous female pop stars of Spanish blood on the walls. There was a strong odor of night-blooming jasmine that Valentino recognized from their first meeting. It wasn't nearly as overpowering as Bozal had described it, except psychologically.

"I think you know why I'm here," he said.

"Who is this man?" said the Oliver clone.

Esperanza snapped her tongue off her teeth. "Don't pretend you're stupider than you are. Valentino, this is Emiliano, my brother."

At close range, the other was close to his sister's age; it was the air of intrigue that had made him look older. His features could be taken for Hispanic or Italian or Middle Eastern, as could Van Oliver/Benny Obrilenski's Semitic ones. The skin wore a slightly olive cast.

"You almost killed me with your car."

"I don't know what you're talking about." His expression was sullen.

"Oh, stop it," Esperanza said. "He knows it was you both times." She turned to Valentino. "He rented the car. If he'd borrowed one of Grandpapa's, it would have given us away. You'd have spotted it following you all the way to that Starbucks."

"'Us'? Why would you want to have me run down?"

"I never wanted that. I told him not to pass too close, just close enough to scare you."

"It scared me. So did what he said afterwards: 'Sorry, buddy. Didn't see you. I will next time.'"

She glared at Emiliano, who shrugged. "I thought it up on

the spot. I couldn't be sure just letting him see my face would do the trick."

Valentino wanted to ask about that face; but it could wait. "Why would you want to scare me? And why did you switch the films?"

She lifted her chin, and in that moment looked exactly like the portrait of her grandmother. In fact, seeing that haughty beauty in the flesh reminded him of someone else, someone he'd seen recently; or had he? Too much had happened in too short a time for him to sort out all his impressions. It was like trying to recall the details of a dream that faded faster the more he tried: fleeing him.

"No one else must ever see that film," she said.

"Why?"

"I can't tell you."

"You might as well. I've figured out the rest. You've seen *Bleak Street*, or at least a photograph of Van Oliver. When you realized your brother looked enough like him to serve as his imposter, you sent him out to frighten me away from the project. Almost running me down wasn't enough. I had to have thought I was being stalked by a ghost. Just to make sure, you dressed him up like Oliver and had him show himself outside The Oracle, where you knew I lived. All that was necessary so I wouldn't press the issue when I found out you'd switched the films."

"That was his idea, the thing at the theater. I told him it was too risky, but he grabbed a coat and hat from Grandpapa's closet and did it anyway."

"I should've done more," Emiliano said. "He didn't scare as easy as you thought." He looked at Valentino. "What she says goes. You can't have that movie."

"Have it your way, then. Don't tell me why. Maybe your grandfather can shed some light." He turned to the door and grasped the knob.

Esperanza dashed across the room and took hold of his arm, tight enough to cause pain. He reacted automatically, seizing both her wrists. All his frustrations went into that grasp. Pain and terror twisted her face. Her brother stepped forward, raising a fist.

"*¡Alto!*" His sister's shout startled him. He stopped. She made no resistance to Valentino's manhandling; she was a rag doll. He let go, ashamed. She rubbed each of her wrists, marked vividly by his fingers. "I can't explain now why we did what we did. That would cause as much harm as if we'd done nothing. If I give you the film, will you promise not to do anything with it and to say nothing to Grandpapa until I can?"

"Why can't you explain now?"

"Not in this house. I'll come to you whenever and wherever you like, and then all will be clear. Maybe it will even change your mind about distributing *Bleak Street* at all." Once again the chin came up and she balled her fists at her sides. "If you refuse, no one will ever see it again. I'll destroy it."

The room filled with silence. Valentino broke it.

"Congratulations."

A crease marred the smooth brown expanse of her forehead. "For what?"

"You finally succeeded in scaring me."

She smiled then; the way she had on his last visit. It unnerved him nearly as much as the certainty that she intended to make good on her threat. This girl—no, this woman—was dangerous, and more to be feared than any ghost.

From under her bed she pulled a cardboard carton containing six unmarked film cans. He didn't wait for her to bring them to him. He swept past her brother, scooped one off the top, opened it, and took out the reel. He unspooled more than a foot of glistening black celluloid and held it up to the light. The first thing he saw was Van Oliver's face, in its proper place and time at last. Hands shaking with relief, he returned everything to the carton and hoisted it under one arm.

At the door he turned back to face Esperanza Bozal. "One week," he said. "It will probably take that long to make a copy. If by then I don't know what this was all about, I'll put the film into general release. Is that understood?"

Brother and sister nodded in unison.

Outside the house, Valentino began to shake again, this time in every limb. He'd managed to run the first successful bluff of his career.

For it was a bluff. He had *Bleak Street*, but could not follow through on his threat to release it if Esperanza didn't hold up her end of the bargain. If he in his turn failed to deliver on his promise to Mark David Turkus and wrap up the Oliver case, he might as well be carrying an empty box.

And then, during the relatively mindless activity of driving back to the secure storage vault at UCLA, it came to him just like that, the answer to everything. It raced through his brain, a surrealist montage of images flashing across his vision like sped-up frames in a film designed to mystify and disturb. It confused, it deranged; it enlightened. When it was finished, he knew what had happened to Van Oliver. Knew it for a certainty.

Now all he had to do was prove it.

27

KYM TRUJILLO CAME out to see him in the entryway of the Motion Picture Country Home. She was petit in a no-nonsense gray pantsuit that gave her free range of motion when pitching in to help nurses and attendants support the weight of ailing residents. She wasn't a dramatic figure like Esperanza Bozal, but with her dark hair piled atop her head and sharp, intelligent features she was as impressive as any beauty from a Spanish opera. Today she was flushed and out of breath.

"I wish you'd called," she told Valentino when he'd explained the reason for his visit. "I might have saved you a trip. We think Roy Fitzhugh had a stroke. We're waiting for the EMS team to come and take him to Cedars of Lebanon."

He felt a stab of concern, as much for the old character actor as for himself and his mission. "Is it bad?"

"There are no good strokes, but it seems to have been mild. It's important we get him into treatment as soon as possible. Every minute counts."

"Could I see him?"

She pursed her lips.

"I shouldn't let you. The regulations are clear about visitors in emergency situations; family only. But he's outlived all his family. You may be able to help keep him calm. He mustn't be upset." Her strong brows drew together. "I mean that. If he shows any sign of agitation, you'll have to leave."

"I promise. I just want to ask him about something he said the last time I was here, information he volunteered. His mind wandered before he could finish."

"I can't tell you if he's lucid or not. It depends on what part of his brain is affected."

"If he isn't, I'll leave. I don't want to be in the way."

"He's in his room. I'm coming along. When the emergency crew comes you'll have to clear out, regardless of his condition."

He thanked her and went with her to Fitzhugh's room. The old man looked small and frail lying under the blankets on his bed. It was difficult to distinguish the outlines of his face from the white pillowcase where his head rested. His pale blue eyes were open and he was breathing evenly with the help of an oxygen tank by the bed and tubes in his nostrils, but he was shaking slightly. Valentino, whose profession placed him frequently in the company of the elderly, recognized it as palsy rather than the effects of a chill. A nurse he'd met before sat in a chair nearby, wearing one of the cheerful floral smocks that had re-placed the stark white uniforms of old. She looked up from her cell phone screen, recognized him, and greeted him with a tight smile.

He remained standing, conscious of Kym Trujillo hovering behind him. He kept his voice low. "It's Valentino, Mr. Fitzhugh. Do you remember me?"

The eyes rolled his direction. A weak smile parted the lips. He wasn't wearing his dentures. "Of course, son. I may be at death's door, but I ain't senile."

Kym said, "Nonsense, Roy. You're as mad as a hatter, but you've got some good years left."

The man in the bed made a dry chuckling sound. It was the kind of banter that existed between a health care professional and a patient who knew better than any doctors.

"Last time we talked about Van Oliver," Valentino said. "You became friends while you were together in *Bleak Street*."

"He made up for a lot. That swish Fletcher said I talked through my schnozz."

They were back in the groove, but he had to prevent the old man from constantly repeating himself and keep him on topic. "You said something about Madeleine Nash, the female lead."

"Maggie. A doll. She used to sing old Spanish songs on the set."

"You said she died."

The eyes misted. Valentino couldn't tell if he was in mourning for an old colleague or in pain. "Yeah. Damn shame."

"I was told she married soon after the film wrapped and left the country."

"Yeah."

Valentino wanted to press it; but he was acutely aware of Kym's eyes boring holes in the back of his neck. He waited. He'd never waited so long for anything, but only a couple of seconds passed before a gray tongue slid along Fitzhugh's pleated lips and he spoke. "I meant after, long after. But still too soon. She never got to see her grandchildren."

"She had grandchildren?"

"Her *grand*children had grandchildren. She missed 'em all. That shouldn't happen to anyone. I hung on this long, and what've I got to show for it? Not a soul to carry on my blood." Something glistened and slid down his cheek, a rivulet tracing the course through a crease.

"You stayed in touch after she went to Europe?"

"Europe?" The old man turned his head a half-inch the visitor's way. The tear had pooled at the corner of his mouth. No others followed it. "Who said she went to Europe?"

Valentino tried to tamp down his excitement. The patient might sense it, become alarmed, and cause him to be ejected.

He realized now he'd had only one source for the Europe story. Everyone else had merely said Madeleine Nash, née Magdalena Novello, left the United States. At that point her vanishing act had been as complete as Van Oliver's, if not as dramatic. All the scattered pieces of a mystery sixty years old were coming together, fitting as snugly as Legos.

He stepped closer to the bed. "Where did she go, if not Europe? Who did she marry?"

"Val." It was Kym.

He stepped back, took a deep breath and let it out. When he spoke his voice was even. "The night Oliver disappeared, you put him in a cab outside Melvin Fletcher's house. Did you get a good look at the driver?"

"Who needs drivers?" Once again, the old man's eyes were as clear as glass beads. "I played one so many times I could drive anyone anywhere." He frowned. "Almost anywhere."

"You made up the taxi story. You drove him yourself."

"Not the whole way. I couldn't show my face in Mexico after that business with my da' when I was a kid."

"After you picked up Oliver you took Nash on board, or someone else did. Who was it? Who met you at the border to take them across?"

A fog slid across the aged eyes. Valentino was losing him. On an impulse he snatched out the photo Mark David Turkus had given him. He held it close to Fitzhugh's face, his thumb next to the obese figure in the background of the cemetery.

The fog cleared. The old man stared. "Holy crap! He got fat."

"Coming through. Out of the way, please."

A man and a woman in uniform with medical patches on the sleeves came in, trundling a stretcher with foldaway wheels. In his fevered state, Valentino hadn't heard the ambulance's siren approaching outside. With Kym Trujillo's hand on his arm he made way, accompanying her out into the corridor.

She let go. "I hope that wasn't a mistake. It sounded pretty important or I wouldn't have let it go on. I guess I got caught up."

"I'm no expert, but I think he'll recover. He's a tough old bird; always was. That kind doesn't give up without a fight."

"I'm sorry he couldn't answer your last question."

"I'm not. I have the answer. All I needed was someone to lead me to it." He slid the picture back into his pocket. As his fingers left it, his eyes went to something in a corner, just past where the corridor opened into the entryway, a volume the size of a family Bible spread open on a wooden lectern. "May I look at the register?"

"Of course. It's open to everyone, you know that."

She left him to supervise Roy Fitzhugh's removal, and Valentino went to the book. He looked at the ruled pages where guests had signed in, adding the dates and times of their visits and occasionally a sentiment. Among them he recognized acquaintances, some of them famous; but none was the one he sought. He turned back the heavy gilt-edged leaves.

And there it was.

A few days ago, he'd have been shocked, then elated. Now he just felt drained. If he'd thought to look there the last time he visited, he could have saved everyone a lot of trouble, most of all himself.

28

A BLACK SEDAN with a hood nearly as long as the Bugatti's (into which his own car could fit without scratching the fenders), narrow running boards, and blazing whitewall tires drifted into the loading zone in front of The Oracle. It was shaped like the spaceship in a Buck Rogers movie, sleek as a shark, every part curving gracefully into every other, with chrome so bright it caught cold fire under the sun of another brilliant day in southern California. Its plate and the insignia above the radiator grille—a gold-and-red enamel escutcheon—identified it as a 1948 Packard.

Valentino, standing in front of the theater's glass-and-nickel doors, was prepared to accept it as the one Van Oliver had driven in throughout *Bleak Street*; it was a graven image, as much as the man himself. At this point in the affair that had begun less than a week earlier in the lobby of the Bradbury Building, he was inclined not to discount anything as impossible.

History repeated itself, never more relentlessly than today.

The rear passenger's door popped open and Ignacio Bozal leaned out, placing a small foot in a crisp brown-and-ivory wingtip onto the running board. The elderly collector had abandoned his shabby house wear for a dove-gray fedora with the brim tugged down rakishly over one eyebrow and a Burberry trench coat knotted rather than tied at the waist, the buckle dangling; the outfit looked more natural on him than it had on his grandson. Valentino caught a glimpse of blue pinstripes, black silk socks that hugged his ankles too snugly to have been held up other than by elastic garters, and a silk necktie decorated with red and black squares set at diamond-shaped angles. He touched the knot as if to secure it, and uncased his store-bought teeth in a neon grin.

"Get in the car."

He made it sound gruff, like a henchman in an old crime film. There was no trace of a Spanish accent.

Valentino asked him where they were going.

"For a ride, what else?"

The archivist didn't laugh. Knowing what he now knew of the man, the answer sounded less like a joke and more like a sinister promise.

Bozal sensed his hesitation. "Around the block a few times; as many as it takes to talk. You never rode in a car like this. I own more'n a hundred, and this one's my favorite. I'm not forgetting the Bugatti. It's got breeding, but this one's got flash." He withdrew his foot and slid to the other side.

It was the second time the archivist had been waylaid by a wealthy and powerful figure in a luxury sedan. As often as he'd seen the scene replayed on-screen, it had never gotten old: until now. Nevertheless he got in.

He recognized the driver. This time he was wearing a chauffeur's uniform. "Where to, Grandpapa?"

"Shut up and drive. I'm still sore at you. Your sister too."

"We were only—"

"Can it!"

Emiliano's face lost its eager-to-please expression. It looked even more like Oliver's; like Bozal's, stripped of the six decades that had taken place since *Bleak Street*. For they were one and the same.

Bozal shook his head. "Can't lay eyes on that kid without feeling someone's walking over my grave. Like looking in a mirror that stopped sixty years ago. Genes are sneaky. They'll go into hiding for generations, then jump out and yell 'Boo!' That what tipped you? I knew it was you when the phone rang. I got the story out of the kids by then. You were smart enough to figure out the rest."

"Not as smart as you think. I should have seen it long before then, but I still didn't get it, not till I could put a little distance between us. The resemblance couldn't have been just coincidence. Neither did all the other signs: Estrella's portrait, painted years after Madeleine Nash left pictures to get married, but the features hadn't changed along with the hairstyle; Esperanza, who could double for Madeleine, except I'd only seen her in black-and-white, not in color or in person; your language— not learned secondhand from watching old movies on TV, but ingrained in you during your time with the New York mob."

They were moving now, cruising through East L.A. neighborhoods he'd never visited. The motor wasn't muted, like the one in Turkus' modern town car, nor did it rumble, like the twelve pistons charging up and down under the Bugatti's hood. It was a powerful throb one could feel in the soles of his feet; the suppressed growl of a savage animal engaged in the stalk.

"Why Estrella, by the way?" Valentino asked. "Why not call her Magdalena?"

"That and Ignacio Bozal were the names on the papers we bought in Tijuana. There wasn't time to have fresh forgeries made. I got used to it. I never could call her Madeleine; that was some PR flak's brainstorm to make her more acceptable to a WASP audience, like when they changed Rita Cansino's last name to Hayworth. She died in Peru in 'sixty-five—Estrella, not Rita. Cancer. That's why I left Acapulco. We had eight good years, but there were too many memories there. The kids— Esperanza and Emiliano's parents and aunts and uncle—were my staff when I opened the hotel. They learned good manners and passed them on; even misplaced loyalty."

"You're Van Oliver. Or do you prefer Benny Obrilenski?"

They were passing down a narrow street walled by blank-faced buildings, *carnicerias* and laundries catering to the local restaurant trade, and probably an indoor *cannabis* farm or two under grow lights. They cast shadows in which only Bozal's bottom teeth showed in a shark's grimace. "I ditched it when I quit the Outfit. Couldn't get used to Van Oliver, though; sounded like a dance-hall gigolo with greased hair and patent-leather pumps."

Valentino had the bizarre feeling he was riding with a stranger, yet one he'd known almost as long as he'd known Bozal. Sometimes—likely from years of careful habit—the man would lapse even now into the border accent, but for the most part it was pure Flatbush: "berl" for "boil," "goil" for "girl," peppered generously with dropped *g*'s and expectorated *t*'s. The clothes, the car, and especially the candor of their conversation had turned the clock back to 1957.

He said, "I knew you'd figured it out last night, when I called to see if Roy was up for a visit and they said he had one. It had to be you. No one else comes to see him these days."

"Did they tell you the rest?"

"Yeah. Call me Madame Zara, I guess. I had a feeling, which is why I called. This morning I was about to check with Cedars of Lebanon when the phone rang and it was you."

"I checked. He's stable. That's all they'd tell me." Valentino went on. "I'd have figured it out a lot earlier if I'd thought to

check the visitors' register the last time I was at the Country
Home. There was your name, the one you're using now. You
signed in three times this year, across from Fitzhugh's name.
Ignacio Bozal had no reason to shoot the breeze with an old
character actor. Van Oliver did."

"How much did he tell you?"

Valentino gave him part of it. Bozal nodded, his aquiline
profile silhouetted in a crack of sunlight between buildings.

"He's slipping, all right. In the old days he wouldn't of said
help if he was drowning."

"He's still cagy. All I got out of him at first was you and
Madeleine Nash went to Mexico, and that only indirectly. You
were the only one who said she went to Europe with her new
husband. You misdirected me twice. You said you got *Bleak
Street* from a private estate sale in Europe."

"I didn't lie about getting it from the editor, just that he was
dead when I got it. I slipped him a grand back in 'fifty-seven.
Just a sentimental souvenir. I met Estrella on that set."

"What about the rest of the money? RKO paid you twenty-
five hundred a week all the time you were on contract. None of
that ever showed up. In the end the authorities concluded you'd
stuck it in a safe-deposit box under an assumed name and never
came back to claim it. That helped confirm the theory you were
murdered."

"It'd just as easily meant I skipped with it; but by then the
press was tired of the case and so were the cops."

Emiliano turned a corner into full sunlight. His grandfather's cheeks showed color for the first time; he never looked
more like Benny Obrilenski, the mob bodyguard who'd struck
Hollywood paydirt. "I earned that money! I wasn't about to kick
back half to that sawed-off runt Mickey Cohen. He was raking
in plenty enough from every racket in this burg without shaking
me down for more.

"That's why we took it on the ankles, Maggie and me." He'd lapsed into Roy Fitzhugh's nickname for Madeleine Nash. "We'd go on making movie after movie, and half of what we got would go into the Mick's pocket. Our only way out was to skip and start over where nobody'd look for us. We sank dry shafts in every tank town and prairie dog hole in Central and South America, picked coffee beans right alongside the hired hands, till we scrounged up the case dough to buy that roach motel in Acapulco and turn it around. You know the rest."

"Not quite. Fitzhugh couldn't cross you into Mexico because of that old smuggling rap. How much did you pay Constantine Turkus to smuggle you across the border?"

"Old Roy sure turned squealer at the end, didn't he?"

"Cut him slack. He was breathing bottled oxygen, waiting for the ambulance to take him to ICU. I ambushed him with a picture of Turkus. It got a reaction."

"I don't hold no grudge. He kept his trap shut all those years when it mattered. I didn't give the Turk much more than cab fare. I think he got a boot out of sneaking U.S. citizens into Mexico instead of the other way around."

"How'd you know him?"

"How do you think? Cohen got him his start busting heads for the studios. I had the lovely job of watching his back while he was doing it."

"That's terrible!"

"You won't get no argument from me. It's why I jumped at the chance when Howard Hughes offered me a contract. Son, you're looking at the only actor who didn't want to be a star. All I wanted was a way out. Maggie—my Estrella—she was a gift from God: Maybe it meant I'd served my time in Perdition."

"You owed her a lot," Valentino said. "Magdalena Novello was a good Spanish tutor."

"She was, but she was raised Castilian. I got the local accent from the natives. I had the coloring to pass, at least with grin-gos. As far as Mexicans were concerned, it was *un asunto de no importa*. They'd been pulling the wool over gringos' eyes for a hundred years."

"Everyone here was satisfied he'd seen the last of Van Oliver. As long as you stayed in character, anyone who happened to rec-ognize you years later might have doubted his own judgment."

It was too warm for a trench coat. The old man unbelted and unbuttoned it, spread it open, and took off his hat. He rested it on his knee and ran a brown hand through his white hair. "I had a couple of close calls, when some mugs came down for vacation. But by then Cohen was in stir for the long haul. I up-graded their rooms, tore up their bills, and they decided they'd made a mistake. Also by then I had some pull in Mexico City. It didn't pay to blow any whistles."

"You sound just like your character in *Bleak Street*."

"You might say I was the first method actor. I started rehears-ing it back in Brooklyn. But I've been playing Bozal so long, I had to climb into this getup to pull off Benny O. I figured you earned a second feature, that's why I offered you the film; get-ting *Greed* on a *quid pro quo* was just an excuse. 'Course I knew you'd dope out the rest. That's *your* M.O."

"But it's not why you agreed to see me today."

"No. If it wasn't for this phony town, I'd of wound up on a slab back East or making gravel in Sing Sing. I only done two things right in my life. You got to see what come of 'em both." He made his crooked grin. "How about them kids? They're smart where it's okay to be dumb and dumb where it counts to be smart. When I ran the picture for her, Esperanza spotted me in the first scene. She'll be a great TV reporter, or whatever it is she's training for. She's got the eye.

"Everything else she found on the Internet, all that bushwah about a great Hollywood mystery. When I let go of *Bleak Street*, she thought I was going screwy, setting myself up for some kind of rap, maybe even a pair of cement overshoes. She's sharp— sharper than Emiliano, for sure—but she let her heart get in the way of her head, protecting me from mugs that were taking a dirt nap before she was born."

His tone dripped with derision, but there was a glint of pride in his eyes. With her brother as an accomplice, she'd nearly brought off a con job that Van Oliver and his old associates could have imagined only in their dreams.

Emiliano called out from the front seat. "The hat and coat were my idea, Grandpapa." His tone was indignant.

"Shut up and drive."

"What about the rest of your family?" Valentino asked. "Do they know?"

Bozal shook his head. "They're bound to, after I'm gone and the biographers nose around long enough to pick up the scent. It won't matter then. I worked a hell of a lot longer getting Bozal right than that character I played in the movie, and anytime you watch an actor put everything into a part and tell him what a good actor he is, it means he screwed up. I'd rather not get bad reviews from my own flesh and blood.

"'Course," he said, "I won't hold you to anything. A deal's a deal, and you held up your end. You got clear title to *Bleak Street* and everything caught up in it."

The archivist made a decision.

"I've got a born-again classic, and an enduring Hollywood mystery to promote it. At this point, a solution would only gum up the works, like if they raised the *Titanic* or identified Jack the Ripper. It could squelch any interest in the film before it sees the light of day."

"You sure? Connie Turkus was camera-shy. If you showed Fitzhugh his picture, you must of got it from his nephew. He won't be too happy to see that can of worms spill out."

"Let me worry about Mark David Turkus, sir. It took me three times as long as it should have, but in the end I'm usually smart where it counts."

Ignacio Bozal—the name Valentino would always associate with him first and foremost—reached over and took his knee in a grip that would crack iron. "My whole film library goes to UCLA two minutes after I croak. There's some stuff there I bet even you never heard of."

Valentino was moved. "*Señor*, when that day comes, I'll make all the arrangements."

Van Oliver put his hat back on, tugging the brim over his left eyebrow, and buttoned and belted his trench coat. His grin was sinister.

"You and what army?"

29

THE CEO OF Supernova International kept his office in the penthouse suite of a former luxury hotel in Century City, where, local legend maintained, mega-producer Darryl F. Zanuck had kept his succession of mistresses during his reign at Twentieth Century Fox.

An armed man in uniform stood sentry before the entrance of the only elevator that went there, beside a white telephone on a fluted pedestal. He took Valentino's name, checked it against a steel clipboard, and lifted the receiver without dialing. He repeated the name to whoever picked up and cradled it. He pressed a button and the doors to the elevator slid open.

The car was done in green marble and red mahogany—invoking Christmas year-round—with the corporation's logo, the eye of a raptor in a circle like a camera lens, embossed on the paneling. As it climbed with no effort on Valentino's part, the piped-in sound system played an orchestration without lyrics that the passenger quickly identified as "Saturday Night at the Movies (Who Cares What Picture We See?)." The illusion of purely emotional, non-commercial devotion to the lively art extended only as far as the room where the company conducted negotiations; that was where the raptor came out, talons first.

The doors opened directly into the suite. It took up the entire top floor without partitions. There was space enough for a vast and glossy desk, a huge table holding up a three-dimensional scale model of a resort on the Riviera, a Nautilus weight-trainer, a complete indoor putting green, and a bank of vintage pinball machines, restored to their original gaudy condition. Windows looked out on Los Angeles in every direction, with a Blu-ray– quality view of the Santa Monica Mountains to the west.

Inside this panoramic display stood a ring of seventy-inch plasma screens, blank at the moment, and inside that a bank of computer monitors on pedestals, a circle within a circle within a circle; this one affording a view of the globe from New York to London to Paris to Moscow to Tokyo to the parking lot at the base of the building, where a man in a uniform identical to the one worn by the guard on the ground floor walked around taking pictures of license plates with a camera phone.

In the center of the last sat Mark David Turkus himself, at a potato chip–shaped desk with nothing on it but a yellow pad and a mechanical pencil, slurping something green through a straw from a tall glass tumbler. Somewhere a mobile phone or tablet hummed incessantly and without response; it could be the president of Pakistan or a pitch for a time-share in Florida for all the attention it got.

As Valentino entered, Turkus rose and came around the desk to offer his hand. He wore an old pullover, tan Dockers, and boat shoes threadbare at the toes; *GQ* had featured him on the cover as "The Man Who Invented Casual Friday."

His grip was tentative, representing years of practice. He'd learned the art of disguise from those ocean predators who camouflaged themselves as harmless creatures.

"I was surprised when you called me so soon," he said. "Does that mean you've made some kind of breakthrough?"

"Some kind."

Turkus indicated a pair of chairs that matched the desk, curved yellow plywood with aluminum frames. "They're more comfortable than they look," he said.

"I'm sure they are, but I don't think this will take long."

"That's unencouraging. Bad news always does."

"That depends on what you consider bad. I know what became of Van Oliver."

The eyes behind the glasses were as flat as washers. "Did my uncle have anything to do with it?"

"Yes."

No change in expression. "And our arrangement stands? You will withhold the information, and *Bleak Street* will remain out of view, with no publicity attached?"

"For the time being."

The barometer in the room dropped. The man carried around his own climate.

"That's not what we agreed on. There was to be no time limit."

"Constantine Venezelos Turkus didn't kill Oliver."

A muscle twitched in the other's cheek; it was invisible unless one looked close. "But you said—"

"I can't give details. I promised someone I wouldn't during the party's lifetime. After that I'll be free to tell you the rest. At that time I'll expect you to honor your part of our bargain and lift the restraining order. The film won't be exhibited and no mention of it will be made to the public until then."

"Can you throw me a bone of any kind?"

Valentino hesitated, as if thinking it over, then nodded. He'd made up his mind on that point before he'd asked for the appointment.

"Whatever else your uncle may have done, killing Van Oliver wasn't one of them. He had nothing to do with the disappearance that could damage your reputation or that of Supernova International."

"Now I'm more curious than ever." But he didn't look confused. Perhaps for the first time in his professional life, an emotion crossed "the Turk's" face; a look of profound relief.

"For some reason I get the impression we'll be meeting again soon," he said.

"Not too soon, I hope. This film's waited sixty years to premiere. A few more won't hurt it."

Something whirred. The elevator doors opened and Teddie Goodman stepped into the room.

She wore yet another of her outlandish outfits, part Theda Bara, part Jane Jetson, an angular metallic thing of scarlet and black supported by eight-inch heels and crowned by a curving spiked comb of blackest jet angling along the part in her hair; for all the world it recalled the tailfin of a German U-boat. She stopped when she spotted Valentino, so abruptly she might have fallen on her face but for her catlike ability to stay on her feet. Her eyes flashed—quite literally—and went from him to Turkus. But she was too accustomed to self-survival—the law of the jungle—to ask the question that was obviously on her mind.

"Miss Goodman. I wasn't aware we'd scheduled a meeting."

Icy calm was restored. "We didn't. I had something to report, something I thought you should know right away. On second thought it can wait."

"If it has anything to do with Mr. Valentino's recent activities, I'm well aware of them. But thank you for your concern."

Her long black lashes lowered in what for her served as a bow. She turned, re-entered the elevator, and faced front. The doors slid shut on her frozen alabaster features.

Valentino broke the silence that followed. "I'll pay for that."

"Possibly. She frightens me, too, sometimes. The guard in the lobby is terrified of her, which is why she comes and goes as she pleases. It can be a valuable property in one's representative. It can also be an intolerable annoyance." He rolled a shoulder. "I can't promise to call her off, short of firing her. She'd be a dangerous character set loose in the wild."

"I'll take my chances. I'd miss her, to be honest."

Once again, Turkus put out his hand.

"Thank you. On behalf of myself, my company, and my family. Thank you."

For the third time in two days, Valentino felt that deceptively mild grip. He'd heard there were close associates who hadn't shaken the billionaire's hand even once.

30

THE ORACLE WAS lit up as if for the 1927 premiere of *Wings*, the first feature to win the Academy Award for Best Picture. Light chased the LED bulbs around the towering marquee, left, right, up, down, and left again, technology's answer to man's quest for the eternal. Searchlights the size of trampolines tinted the bellies of clouds in cotton-candy colors, the shafts crisscrossing like swords in combat. Guests in full evening dress crossed the red carpet under the glittering canopy, admiring the barbaric splendor of ancient civilizations, mythic beasts, and pagan deities restored to life in gilt, plaster, and resin; all the illusionary, elusive, over-the-top art of the Hollywood Dream Factory.

Harriet Johansen was first to arrive, in a silver lamé gown that clung to her slim athletic frame and reflected the light in flat sheets. She kissed Valentino and pointed the corner of her clutch purse at the man who'd taken her gold-bordered pass, in a tuxedo that could only have been cut to his massive measure. A black velvet band of mourning encircled one sleeve.

"Wherever did you find him?"

Valentino was standing next to the vacant ticket booth wearing a white dinner jacket.

"His name's Vivien, believe it or not. He came to me three days ago, saying he owed me a favor. He doesn't—I was just a catalyst—but I couldn't pass up the opportunity. He's already turned away a dozen people who thought this was a public event."

"I can't think how they made that mistake. The place only looks like the World's Fair." She looked at the man again. "He reminds me of someone."

"Only if you've seen *The Incredible Hulk*."

"The TV show? Loved it. In re-runs, I mean. Is he—?"

"Not Lou Ferrigno. Leave it to a forensics expert to recognize a stunt double after all these years."

She beamed. "How can I help?"

"Stand beside me. That way no one will notice I borrowed this outfit from the Hallmark Channel."

"You look like Rick Blaine." She studied his face.

"Just by coincidence; it was the only thing available. I won't play it again, Sam. This time."

She was looking at the next arrivals. "I think I just got up-staged."

Fanta Broadhead approached, her arm linked with her husband's. She was a glittering mermaid in sparkling green sequins and a white wrap that would have passed for ermine if she didn't do *pro bono* work for the ASPCA.

The host kissed her on the cheek. "You look wonderful."

"This old thing?" She hugged Harriet. "You clean up well, too."

Valentino shook Broadhead's hand. "So do you."

The professor tugged at his starched collar. In a black tuxedo with onyx studs he might have passed for a truck driver at his daughter's wedding. "Third time I've worn the monkey suit, thanks to you. I should've suspected what Fanta was up to when she talked me into buying it instead of renting one for the hitching post. I thought she intended to bury me in it."

"We've heard it all before, old man," said his wife. "I told you when you proposed I wasn't going to spend the rest of my life in sensible shoes and a tailored suit like all the rest of the faculty wives. That meant dressing you up so it wouldn't look like I checked you out of a hotel for transients. And just for the record, *I* proposed to *you*."

"I said I'd think about it. I was still thinking when you dragged me to the cake-tasting."

"You forget a lawyer never asks a question she doesn't know the answer to," she said.

Broadhead turned to survey the small group lined up behind them. "Not much of a turnout. I warned you when this whole thing started you'll never lure people away from their living rooms and Netflix."

"Did you look at the invitation?" Valentino said.

"'Admit two,' along with the lame tease of a sneak premiere. What part of 'grand opening' did you not understand?"

"It's the grandest company I could have wished for."

Fanta turned toward the centerpiece of the ornate lobby, an oil portrait of a hauntingly lovely brunette in its original Deco frame, securely sealed in a shadow box made of beveled glass. "It looks even better than it did in the Bradbury."

"I hoped it would. Mounting it in that case cost me four hundred dollars. Anytime someone offers you a gift, make sure you can afford it."

"You know," she said, "I like it more than the one they used in the film."

"Meaning no disrespect to a beautiful actress, that's because the one Preminger had made looks like Gene Tierney. This one looks like Laura, the unachievable ideal. That's an impossible undertaking for any mortal casting director, no matter how talented. Vera Caspary preferred it to the other; but what did she know? She only wrote the novel the picture was based on."

"Will Bozal be coming?" Broadhead said.

"He declined. He's in Tuscany, scouting locations for a theme park he wants to build. It seems the Catholic Church liked the idea well enough to clear it with the authorities. Anyway, he's seen the picture."

Fanta said, "What *is* the picture, by the way? *Casablanca*? Harriet told me about that."

He smiled. "Not *Casablanca*."

"He won't even tell *me*," Harriet said.

Still smiling, he turned and opened the embossed bronze door that led into the auditorium.

Henry Anklemire was next in line, in his purple smoking jacket and a green-and-yellow-striped bow tie. "Snazzy joint, kiddo. You could put up the Lost Tribe of Israel in a room this size and still have space for a pool table."

"Good of you to come, Henry. No hard feelings about what we discussed, I hope."

"What the heck. Don't take it the wrong way, but I didn't really think you could do it. Land on Mars, maybe, but rip the lid off a case the cops gave up on before you was born? Meshugana!"

"You can't win 'em all."

Anklemire patted his arm. "Better luck next time. Just let me know when I can go to work on the pitch. I'll come up with something."

"I will."

"Popcorn's free, right?"

"I hired a caterer. You can have shrimp and lobster if you like."

"Just so long as you don't rat me out to Temple Beth Shalom." He adjusted his toupee and strutted through the door.

Harriet smiled after him. "No one's *that* Jewish. I bet he's a closet Methodist."

"Nobody knows Henry," Valentino said. "He's entirely a creature of manufacture: Mr. Whipple out of Betty Crocker by way of Morris the Cat. They were all born on a drawing board on Madison Avenue."

"You're a puzzle yourself. For someone who was so determined to get to the bottom of the Van Oliver case, you seem to have dropped it like a hot lightbulb. What'd I tell you about keeping secrets?"

"This one isn't mine to share," he said. "When it is, you'll be the first to know."

A new voice interrupted the conversation.

"I like what you've done with the place. Ditching the skeleton was a good start."

Valentino straightened at the sight of the tall redhead in the shimmering blue gown; it was part surprise, part force of habit whenever he found himself face-to-face with an old adversary. She looked more statuesque than ever in six-inch heels and pearls. For the first time it struck him that she was a remarkably beautiful woman, something she managed to camouflage through fierce intelligence and ruthless efficiency on the job.

"Sergeant Clifford. I'm so glad you came."

"I can tell. I haven't seen that look on anybody's face since I slapped the cuffs on a former child star with blood on his shirt. This is my husband, Ray. He's a criminal attorney. We only fight when he's cross-examining me in court."

He shook the hand of a stout, ruddy-faced man whose head barely cleared his wife's bare shoulders. "Don't listen to her. She

was thrilled when she got the invitation. The last time she got
to gussy up, it was in dress blues with a black band on her
shield."

"I object," she said.

"Overruled."

Valentino said, "Enjoy the show."

On her way past, Clifford bent to his ear. "When can I expect a signed statement? I'm not talking about Ivy Lane. The
Oliver file's still open downtown."

Valentino hesitated. "I'll keep you posted."

Harriet said, "Did you do as I suggested and invite Teddie
Goodman?"

"I decided against it, for reasons of delicacy. I'll tell you
about it someday."

When everyone was seated, the lights came down and a bar
of white light struck the screen.

Valentino had borrowed the UCLA projectionist for the
evening, along with some footage from the secure storage vault.
Following Bugs Bunny and a travelogue on the virtues of the
Republic of Cuba came a black-and-white newsreel showing
Queen Elizabeth II offering a gloved hand to President Eisenhower. Valentino, seated in the center balcony looking down on
the screen, felt Harriet stirring restlessly in the adjoining seat.
She knew he always insisted on matching the dates of vintage
features with vintage films.

When the RKO tower went to black and the title card came
on, she whispered, "I should've known."

She was a trained close observer, more so than he, for all
his education in the visual arts. Halfway through the opening scene—the anti-hero's dramatic entrance, stepping down
from the chair car of a westbound train—she tensed, shifted
positions, turned her head partly Valentino's way, stopped,

watched a minute more, then leaned across the armrest they shared.

"That looks like—"

He shushed her, whispered: "You know how I feel about talking during a movie."

A WORD FROM VALENTINO

The images are iconic, and uniquely American: The pulled-down hat brim, the rumpled trench coat, the cigarette dangling from the corner of a lip; the feline creature in the tight dress, deadlier than the male; gigantic shadows on the brick wall of an alley, a piece of the city that has broken loose and lodged in a place of eternal night.

Like most native culture, this cinematic sub-genre (commonly bracketed between 1945 and 1958, although there are notable exceptions as far back as 1931 and as recent as 1967) came about through several influences: in this case, post-war disillusionment, the erosion of faith in governments and institutions, and men's concerns about women's independence earned during wartime employment in the defense industry. The final touch came from Jewish and dissident filmmakers in flight from the Holocaust, bringing with them the expressionistic camera angles, Cubist sets, and themes outlawed as "decadent" by Nazi Germany. Ironically, the U.S. studios' strict censorship code, which prohibited overt violence, sexual situations, and sins unpunished, led to a subtlety of symbols and expression that still resonates today. Like the steam-engine, this was a development whose time had come. All it needed was a name.

That came from French critics who, when the embargo on U.S. films was lifted after the Liberation, saw the films back-to-back, observed the consistency of theme, and cried, film *noir!*;* literally, "black film." It was raw, it was unapologetic, and it told the truth: In the words of the narrator of *Detour* (1945), "Fate, or some mysterious force, can put the finger on you or me for no good reason at all."

Twenty-first-century audiences, accustomed to the frantic pace of superhero, sci-fi, and other hypermodern productions adapted from graphic novels (comic books, to an earlier generation) may lose patience with the oblique motives and slow buildup of suspense to be found in classic *noir,* but a steady diet—excluding any movie whose special-effects credits run almost into the next showing—should convert all but the hopeless. These films were made for grown-ups, assuming intelligence on the part of their viewers, and an attention span longer than a high-five.

The effect of *noir* can't be described in words, only images: A man pushed out a high window, falling away from the camera; the orgasmic leer on a psychopath's face in the act of murder; the gold anklet worn by a scheming woman descending a staircase; a child-killer pleading for mercy on his knees before a jury of ordinary cutthroats; a cynical detective falling in love with the portrait of the woman whose murder he's investigating. These are not images you watch; you breathe them in like gas—odorless, colorless, inescapable, and lethal.

Then come back for another whiff.

---

* With help from French publisher Gallimard's "*Serie Noire*," which brought translations of American crime novels to Europe.

CLOSING CREDITS

The list of *noir* films currently in circulation, previously over-looked, just plain forgotten, and dismissed as lost is constantly in flux, just as the material between covers that informs, analyzes, and educates the reader on this singular movement in cinema history is too vast to contain in the backmatter of one book. The revolution in home viewing that began with the VCR and exploded when DVDs came along has rescued thousands of features from storage vaults where many have remained for more than a century. Hundreds of *noir* entries have come to light, including titles previously unknown by accomplished film historians. The following sources are recommended (along with general works on film that were employed in researching *Indigo*):

BIBLIOGRAPHY

Alton, John. *Painting with Light*. Berkeley: University of California, 1995.

I can't praise this wonderful book too highly. The cinematographer whose use of contrast and composition gave *noir* its signature look shares with us the secrets of his genius. At a time when he and his colleagues were generally dismissed as mere technicians, Alton (*T-Men, Raw Deal, He Walked by Night, Border Incident, The Big Combo*) recognized the central part his craft played in the creation of this unique and powerful art. The chapter headings alone are enough to sell the book: "Hollywood Photography"; "Motion Picture Illumination"; "Mystery Lighting"; "Symphony in Snow," etc. It was first published in 1949, at the height of his career. The introduction to this new edition by film critic and documentarian Todd McCarthy is excellent.

Baker, J. J., editor. *Film Noir: 75 Years of the Greatest Crime Films.* New York: *Life,* 2016.

Decades after its demise as a weekly staple, this most American of magazine publishers remains current with its special issues examining single subjects. There's nothing new here, but I have to applaud this institution for bringing film *noir* back into the spotlight, educating a new generation with this sumptuously illustrated primer.

Clarens, Carlos. *Crime Movies.* New York: Norton, 1980.

This is an early entry in the post-1970s renaissance of material on the crime thriller. The twelve-page chapter titled "Shades of Noir" alone contains tons of material on the evolution of the sub-genre from the novels of Dashiell Hammett, Raymond Chandler, James M. Cain, et al, through their screen adaptations, and films inspired by the adaptations, more than you'll find in many whole books.

Kaplan, E. Ann. *Women in Film Noir.* London: British Film Institute, 1978.

This study was heavily revised in 1980 and reprinted many

times. The essays, including the title piece by Janey Place, establish *noir* as an empowering influence on behalf of womankind and actresses; evil these characters may be, but their superior intelligence and determination broke them out of the stereotypical roles of Good Girl, Tramp, Tomboy, Victim. None of *these* ladies stood by wringing her hands while a man took care of business.

Mainon, Dominique and James Ursini. *Femme Fatale: Cinema's Most Unforgettable Lethal Ladies.* Milwaukee: Limelight, 2009.

From Theda Bara (the original Teddie Goodman) to Catherine Zeta-Jones, Mainon and Ursini provide a running tally of the Jezebels who have led their leading men (sometimes with their willing cooperation) to their doom. Exquisitely illustrated in glossy black-and-white and color plates, this one makes the descent into hell seem worth it.

Mordden, Ethan. *The Hollywood Studios: House Style in the Golden Age of the Movies.* New York: Knopf, 1988.

A general guide, essential in recognizing the trademark styles, business practices, and creative decisions of RKO, Warner Brothers, Universal, and United Artists; not forgetting those plucky independents whose B-movie budgets forced them to stay on point and make the best artistic use of the materials at hand, with results so impressive even their deep-pocket competitors co-opted their methods.

Muller, Eddie. *The Art of Noir: The Posters and Graphics from the Classic Era of Film Noir.* Woodstock, NY: Overlook, 2002.

Muller, a fixture on TV's Turner Classic Movies, frequent commentator on DVD releases, and a co-organizer of *noir* film festivals, knows his stuff. *The Art of Noir,* just one of his many books on this subject, is a coffee-table gem: 279 slick, folio-size pages of full-color reproductions of the advertising art that helped define the form, with capsule commentaries on the films themselves.

Silver, Allain and James Ursini, eds. *Film Noir Reader, Vols. 1–3.* New York: Limelight, 1996, 1999, 2002.

Scholarly, but by no means pedantic, this series takes us from Raymond Borde and Etienne Chaumeton's seminal 1955 French essay "Towards a Definition of Film *Noir*" through Philip Gaines's "*Noir* 101," published in 1999. The third volume, co-edited by Robert Porfiro, provides illuminating interviews with period filmmakers.

Silver, Allain, Elizabeth Ward, James Ursini, and Robert Porfiro, eds. *Film Noir: The Encyclopedia.* New York: Overlook, 2010.

Fanatics have awaited this new edition for years; in the meantime we had to content ourselves with occasional "update" volumes. This one makes use of colossal numbers of newly released DVDs, essays, and an expanded panel of experts to chronicle nearly every title in the *noir* canon (inexplicable snubs: *Murder, Incorporated, Tight Spot*), along with production notes, period reviews, and modern commentary. You may not agree with them all the time, but you'll respect their dedication. A new section analyzes neo-*noir* remakes and originals. The word "indispensable" is overused, but if any source deserves it, this does. If it's not on your shelves, you're not one of us.

Silver, Allain and James Ursini. *The Noir Style.* Woodstock, NY: Overlook, 1999.

Another coffee-table treasure, lavishly illustrated in black-and-white, tracing the evolution of the genre from *Scarface* (1931) through *The Silence of the Lambs* (1991), tying in the neo-*noir* movement that began in the 1970s. It makes a *prima facie* case against director James Spader's preposterous claim that this timeless school of moviemaking is a "historical" artifact, as dead as King Duncan.

Tuska, Jon. *Dark Cinema: American Film Noir in Cultural Perspective.* Westport, Conn.: Greenwood, 1984.

Treatises don't get more scholarly than this. Tuska's exhaustive research draws a straight line from Euripides and Shakespeare to Clifford Odets, exhibiting a trend that explains mankind's fascination with the flawed heroes and heroines of tragedy. This historian's intimacy with many Hollywood idols enlivens his narrative, preventing it from sinking into a morass of cant.

FILMOGRAPHY

Here are some essentials; don't stop there.

The Big Combo. Directed by Joseph Lewis, written by Philip Yordan, starring Cornel Wilde, Richard Conte, Brian Donlevy, Jean Wallace, Robert Middlelton, Lee Van Cleef, Earl Holliman, and Helen Walker. Allied Artists, 1955.

This one rides on strong performances and John Alton's genius behind the camera. Wilde's detective sets out to nail mob boss Conte by tracking down the mysterious Alicia (Walker, as Conte's forcibly institutionalized ex-wife: "I'd rather be insane and alive than sane—and dead"). Van Cleef and Holliman's sadistic henchmen are patently homosexual; Lewis gets around censorship standards simply by letting them share a bedroom and some effeminate characteristics; who can object to that? Brian Donlevy's death, mowed down by machine guns in eerie silence because Conte has taken away his hearing aid, is one of the iconic scenes in *noir*. Conte shone in gangster roles, managing to be evil and emotionally vulnerable at the same time (his final appearance, as Don Barzini in *The Godfather,* has touches of sardonic humor, and his slaying on the steps of a church echoes James Cagney's at the end of *The Roaring Twenties*). Censors decried Lewis' push-the-envelope love scene with Wallace and missed the homoerotic subtext mentioned above.

The Big Heat. Directed by Fritz Lang, written by Sydney Boehm (based on the novel by William P. McGivern), starring Glenn Ford, Gloria Grahame, Jocelyn Brando, Alexander Scourby, Lee Marvin, Jeanette Nolan. Columbia, 1953.

Lang, Billy Wilder's fellow émigré from Nazi Germany, is most often praised for his silent *Metropolis*; but even restored and remastered, that one creaks (and Blu-ray is wasted on productions that predate the technology), while *The Big Heat* grows stronger with each viewing. It's a simple revenge tale: Gangsters kill detective Ford's wife, so he quits the corrupt force and sets out to destroy the mob. He seethes throughout, just under the boiling point. Marvin's street soldier is a sadistic coward, deliriously easy to hate, Nolan as the widow of a bent cop is a heartless schemer, and Graham—*noir's* best *femme fatale* by a league—stands out as Marvin's kittenish, victim-turned-avenger moll. (To Nolan: "We're sisters under the mink.") McGivern was one of the best of the postwar hard-boiled novelists, and the film is faithful to the book.

Born to Kill. Directed by Robert Wise, written by Eve Greene and Richard Macauley (based on the novel *Deadlier than the Male* by James Gumm), starring Claire Trevor, Lawrence Tierney, Walter Slezak, Audrey Long, Elisha Cook, Jr. RKO, 1947.

Trevor's amoral, Tierney's a psychopath. They marry: A match made in hell. Trevor gave up A-list stardom at MGM for roles she could get her teeth into, thanks be to God. Tierney (no relation to Gene), whose cruel good looks made him a convincing remorseless killer (and whose off-screen persona mirrored his screen image, as late as 1992's *Reservoir Dogs*), was never less human. Cook excels as his stooge, constantly trying to govern Tierney's rage (FYI: He fails). The presence of one of these players in a crime movie screams *noir*; all three settle the point.

The Dark Corner. Directed by Henry Hathaway, written by Jay Dratler and Bernard Schoenfield (based on the story by Leo Rosten), starring Mark Stevens, Lucille Ball, Clifton Webb, William Bendix, Kurt Krueger. 20th Century Fox, 1946.

Ex-con P.I. Stevens is framed for murder; simple premise, diabolic plot. Future TV megastar Ball sparkles as the take-charge Girl Friday, and the process shot in which Bendix falls to his death away from the camera is a honey.

Detour. Directed by Edgar Ulmer, written by Martin Goldsmith, starring Tom Neal, Ann Savage, Claudia Drake, Edmund MacDonald. PRC, 1945.

The fatalistic premise, sharp use of light and shadow, and Ulmer's skill in whipping a Z budget into an A-minus production have made this a staple of the form; but for me, it's a prime example of what some call "dumb s**t noir." Hey, Einstein! Next time you want to stop someone (Savage, whose name fits this character) from incriminating you over the phone, skip the tug-of-war and rip the box out of the wall on your side of the door!

Double Indemnity. Directed by Billy Wilder, written by Wilder and Raymond Chandler (based on the novella by James M. Cain), starring Fred MacMurray, Barbara Stanwyck, Edward G. Robinson. Paramount, 1944.

The jewel in the crown. Insurance salesman MacMurray

allows himself to be drawn by Stanwyck into a plot to murder her husband for his life insurance. A tale of seduction, betrayal, reprisal, and karma, with superior pace and some of the best dialogue in pictures, courtesy of Chandler, who made all the improvements on the overheated novella. MacMurray, Hollywood's textbook nice guy, retains our sympathy throughout, in spite of (and maybe because of) his complicity in homicide. Stanwyck's the ultimate *femme fatale*, cunning and ruthless, and Robinson's insurance investigator steals every scene he's in. The film was nominated for three Academy Awards: Best picture, script, direction. No other *noir* ever came close.

The Glass Key. Directed by Stuart Heisler, written by Jonathan Latimer (based on the novel by Dashiell Hammett), starring Brian Donlevy, Veronica Lake, Alan Ladd, William Bendix. Paramount, 1942.

Critics who dismiss Alan Ladd as a "pint-size tough guy" are probably compensating for their own inadequacies; he was taller than James Cagney and a better actor than John Garfield, who was just Paul Muni with angst. Study the emotionally charged scene with William Bendix, who last time he got together with Ladd beat him nearly to death: Try to keep your eyes off Ladd, delivering his lines through his teeth and playing with the whiskey bottle he's obviously planning to use to crown Bendix (he never does, making the tension all the more unbearable). The diminutive team of Ladd and Lake in several films set them apart as the Astaire and Rogers of *noir*. (Cheers also to Joel and Ethan Coen's 1990 *Miller's Crossing*, an uncredited remake that's more faithful to Hammett's vision, if not specifically to his plot.)

Kiss of Death. Directed by Henry Hathaway, written by Ben Hecht and Charles Lederer (from a story by Eleazar Lipsky), starring Victor Mature, Brian Donlevy, Coleen Gray, Richard Widmark, Karl Malden. 20th Century Fox, 1947.

How do you make a stool pigeon sympathetic? Easy: Cast Richard Widmark as his antagonist. Mature's solid, square build sets him apart from the weasely squealers who are almost invariably whacked in phone booths ratting out his pals to the cops, while Widmark's slithery, jittery, giggling killer makes you want to squash him like a bug; if only you had the guts. For Tommy Udo (Widmark), shoving an old lady in a wheelchair down a long flight of stairs is like skipping rope, right down to the orgasmic giggle.

Laura. Directed (and produced) by Otto Preminger, written by Jay Dratler, Samuel Hoffenstein, Ring Lardner, Jr., and Betty Reinhardt (based on Vera Caspary's novel), starring Gene Tierney, Dana Andrews, Clifton Webb, Vincent Price, Judith Anderson. 20th Century Fox, 1944.

Glossy, glamorous, and psychologically ambiguous, *Laura* is the Tiffany of *noir*. Scintillating socialite Tierney, molded Pygmalion-fashion from common clay by catty columnist Webb (a tour-de-force performance by this second-string Claude Rains), murdered in her penthouse apartment, becomes the obsession of homicide detective Andrews, who falls in love with her through her backstory, personal effects, and above all her painted portrait. The hard-bitten cop, who when asked if he'd ever been in love replies, "A dame in Washington Heights got a fox fur out of me once," turns hostile when the "victim" reappears from the dead (the corpse isn't hers), and fixes upon her as the principal suspect, possibly in a fit of seeming betrayal. The cast is superb, with amusing and poignant support from cad Price and jaded *doyenne* Anderson. Unlike some suspensers that attempt to jam romance into the plot, *Laura*'s romantic subtext is both integral and inevitable.

The Maltese Falcon. Directed by John Huston, written by John Huston (based on the novel by Dashiell Hammett), starring Humphrey Bogart, Mary Astor, Peter Lorre, Barton MacLane, Sydney Greenstreet, Ward Bond, Jerome Cowan, Elisha Cook, Jr. Warner, 1941.

I confess I was disappointed the first time I saw this lodestone of the genre. Since it broke ground, its many imitators made it seem like nothing new. Later I came to appreciate it for Bogart's spot-on cynicism (armor to protect his firm integrity), Lorre's eel-like smarm, Cook's murderous adolescence, and Greenstreet's chortling villainy. Astor comes off too mature and sophisticated to convince us that Bogart's Sam Spade is truly in love with her; but Huston's insistence on breaking with Hollywood tradition and actually filming the novel (two earlier attempts had strayed and consequently failed at the box office), set a precedent that, praise be, is still with us.

Murder, My Sweet. Directed by Edward Dmytryk, written by John Paxton (based on the novel *Farewell, My Lovely,* by Raymond Chandler), starring Dick Powell, Claire Trevor, Anne Shirley, Otto Kruger, Mike Mazurki. RKO, 1944.

Powell, after an unsuccessful bid for the part that went to Fred MacMurray in *Double Indemnity,* made a triumphant switch here from lightweight musicals to crime dramas. The neon-lit opening, with Mazurki's apish face reflected enormously in Powell's night-backed window, gave the genre its seductive look. (For a more direct interpretation of Chandler's novel, snag Dick Richards' 1975 *Farewell, My Lovely*; Mitchum, born to play Philip Marlowe, should have done it twenty years earlier—but, hey, it's Mitchum! opposite slinky Charlotte Rampling, who never evoked Lauren Bacall so closely again; nor, for that matter, did Bacall. But enjoy Powell's brash Marlowe, and yet another of Trevor's delicious tramps.)

Out of the Past. Directed by Jacques Tourner, written by Geoffrey Homes (Daniel Mainwaring), Frank Fenton, and James M. Cain (based on Mainwaring's novel *Build My Gallows High*), starring Robert Mitchum, Jane Greer, Kirk Douglas, Rhonda Fleming, Steve Brodie, Virginia Huston, Dickie Moore. RKO, 1947.

This is *numero uno* on most aficionados' lists. I agree as to the players: Vintage Mitchum, that sleepy, dangerous panther; Greer's smoldering beauty; Douglas establishing his chummy-snake brand of perfidy early in his career; and Moore's eloquent silence as Mitchum's mute confidant. It was a mistake, however, to place Fleming's and Greer's scenes in San Francisco back-to-back, as two brunettes in updos (Greer's hair is down on her shoulders everywhere else), confusing these two scheming females in the viewer's mind and snarling the plot. That said, this is fine Greek tragedy, in which a single lapse in judgment leads to five violent deaths. This is what would have befallen Bogart's Spade had he refused to "send over" Brigid O'Shaughnessy in *Falcon* (although with due respect to Astor's charms, I'd have a harder time dumping Greer).

Pitfall. Directed by André de Toth, written by William and André de Toth and Karl Kamb (based on the novel by Jay Dratler), starring Dick Powell, Lizabeth Scott, Jane Wyatt, Raymond Burr, Byron Barr. United Artists, 1948.

Powell's an insurance investigator and a restless family man trying to collect insured goods stolen by jailed thief Barr and given to girlfriend Scott. Powell and Scott begin an extramarital affair, to the intense displeasure of sleazy private eye Burr, in one of Burr's most threatening "heavy" (physically and figuratively) turns. To satisfy the Production Code, Powell must pay for his infidelity; but his penalty is the crux of a riveting and completely plausible plot. Wyatt, best remembered as Robert

Young's faithful *hausfrau* in TV's *Father Knows Best*, excels as the dishonored wife: first furious, then defensively manipulative, finally resolved to pick up the pieces of a shattered marriage. (Powell's best, bitterest line: "How does it feel to be a decent, respectable married man?")

Too Late for Tears. Directed by Byron Haskin, written by Roy Huggins (based on his novel), starring Lizabeth Scott, Don DeFore, Dan Duryea, Arthur Kennedy, Kristine Miller, Barry Kelley. United Artists, 1949.

Scott and Duryea are the dream team. Her Jane Palmer will sacrifice anything, even her spouse (another solid contribution from the undervalued Kennedy), for the satchel of cash that accidentally falls in her lap. The magic moment comes when Duryea, whose screen persona has been aptly described as "a lady-slapping heel"—a nasty gigolo always out for the main chance—realizes that when it comes to pitiless determination, Scott is way out of his league.

Touch of Evil. Directed by Orson Welles, written by Welles (based on the novel *Badge of Evil* by Whit Masterson), starring Charlton Heston, Janet Leigh, Orson Welles, Joseph Calleia, Akim Tamiroff, Marlene Dietrich, Dennis Weaver, Mercedes McCambridge, Zsa Zsa Gabor. Universal, 1958.

Gloriously overheated, with enough deep-seared images to support a dozen *noirs*, Welles's best film after *Citizen Kane* makes full use of the innovations he brought to Hollywood (and for which the industry never forgave him) to show this movement out with a bang. Heston's often ridiculed for playing a Mexican, but his dignified aspect and stony resolve to see justice prevail do more honor to the race than so many Hispanics habitually cast as moronic bandits and comic relief. This is a stunning double-play, with Welles bringing all his genius to the direction and also to the part of the loathsome Detective Quinlan. Leigh as victim is far from helpless, Weaver's bat-s**t motel manager is unique in cinema, and Dietrich's border-town madam provides the Greek chorus. Despite what's been said about the so-called "director's cut"—ostensibly based posthumously on Welles's production notes—watch the theatrical version first. That brilliant opening long take is more dramatic with the title crawl included.

White Heat. Directed by Raoul Walsh, written by Ivan Goff and Ben Roberts (based on a story by Virginia Kellogg), starring James Cagney, Virginia Mayo, Edmond O'Brien, Margaret Wycherly, Steve Cochran, Fred Clark. Warner, 1949.

Cagney's masterpiece. His Cody Jarrett, a Dillinger-type gangleader, albeit saddled with paranoid/schizophrenic tendencies and the mother of all Oedipus complexes, is nevertheless charismatic and impossible not to root for; especially with undercover cop O'Brien worming his way into his confidence in order to betray him. This is what would have come of Tom Powers, Cagney's breakthrough role in *The Public Enemy*, had he survived Prohibition. Mayo is *fatale* as all get-out as his floozy wife, Cochran unforgettable as his rival for gang leadership. Raoul's past as a director of classic westerns soups up the action from the opening shot of a charging locomotive all the way to the explosive finish, leaving no place to go out for popcorn.

So many more *noirs*; and our running time is so short. Happy hunting!